Make-Believe Wedding

Make-Believe Wedding

A MONTANA BORN BRIDES NOVELLA

SARAH MAYBERRY

TULE
PUBLISHING

DEDICATION

With thanks to Jane Porter and the other amazing authors who make up the Montana Born stable. Your generosity, support, ideas and collaboration have made writing this book an absolute joy.

Thanks also to Chris, who is the reason why I keep telling friends-to-lovers stories over and over, because he is my best friend as well as the hottest man I know, and may it ever be so. I love you, husband of mine.

Dear Reader,

Writing this book was a joy from beginning to end. It's not often a writer can say that – sometimes it feels as though you're chiselling every word from granite – but *Make-Believe Wedding* was so much fun to write, I couldn't wait to sit down at the computer every day. I loved imagining my way into the world of Andie and Heath and giving them the happy every after they both needed and deserved. It was especially good fun to try to touch base with other characters from the previous eight Montana Born Great Wedding Giveaway novellas, and to finish up with a wedding.

I hope you enjoy reading about Andie's long unrequited love for Heath, and his slow awakening to the fact that his oldest friend's little sister is more than just a good friend and great employee. Thank you for allowing me to have one of the most fun, rewarding experiences of my writing career.

All the best, and happy reading,

Sarah Mayberry

Chapter One

Valentine's Day, Marietta, Montana.

ANDIE BENNETT WATCHED the couple on the dance floor with unabashed longing. Normally she'd be more discreet about her yearning, but tonight she'd had too much wine to care if anyone noticed she was wildly, passionately, pathetically in love with Heath McGregor, despite the fact that he was her older brother's best friend.

Oh, and her employer. Mustn't forget that he was also the one who signed her paycheck every week.

Marietta's inaugural Valentine's Day ball swirled around her, the locals of their small Montana town having dusted off their best suits and gowns for the occasion. Pink fairy lights hung from the decorative ceiling of The Graff Hotel's ballroom, and red and pink decorations dotted the tables and draped the walls.

If you were here with someone you loved, someone you planned on taking home to your bed, it would probably be really romantic.

Andie's gaze slid to the woman in Heath's arms, another

petite, buxom brunette in a long line of petite, buxom brunettes. What did her brother call them again? *Pocket rockets.* Right. Heath liked his women small and curvy and dark-haired, always had, apparently always would. Which was great news for the woman circling the dance floor with him right now, but bad news for Andie.

At five eleven, she stood almost eye-to-eye to Heath's six foot one, and she was about as curvy as a bean pole. Her chest was almost flat – on a good day, if she were feeling optimistic and the bra manufacturer were generous, she was a B-cup – her hips boyishly slim. The only thing she had going for her was that she had long legs.

Some men liked long legs. Not Heath. Heath liked boobs. And dark, shiny hair, instead of wishy-washy blonde blah, and brown eyes instead of plain-old blue.

But she knew all this. She'd known this for thirteen years, ever since puberty had hit and she'd looked at her brother's best friend with new eyes and known that he was The One. Sadly, he hadn't been struck with the same realization. He thought of Andie as the little sister he never had, which had been fine when she was a teenager, but really sucked now that she was a woman, with a woman's wants and needs.

God, how she wanted and needed Heath McGregor. She wanted to tear his black suit from his shoulders and pounce on him. She wanted to ravage that wicked mouth of his, with its fuller, decadent lower lip with smiley corners. She wanted to rub her cheek against his stubble-shaded jaw, and run her hands over his broad, strong chest, and curve her palms over that perfect, hard round ass of his...

She made a sound that might have been a whimper and reached for her wine glass. The people on her table had left long ago, getting up to dance or circulate and catch up with friends, abandoning her to her drinking and yearning. It didn't matter, she didn't know any of them. She'd bought a single ticket to the dance, and the organizers had plonked her on a table with a bunch of other misfits.

To think, not two hours ago she'd been standing in her bedroom, convinced that tonight was going to be the night that changed everything. She'd actually been nervous with excitement, she'd bought into her own bull so much. She'd been to the hairdresser and had her hair cut and highlighted and woven into a sophisticated up-do. She'd spent a fortune on a slinky navy-blue dress from a ridiculously exclusive boutique in Bozeman. She'd shoe-horned her poor feet into these stupid high heels and sprayed her body with perfume and followed the instructions from the girl at the make-up counter at Macy's to make her eyes smoky. She'd even stuck on a set of false eyelashes to "make her eyes really pop".

She'd looked as good as she was ever going to, a million miles from the jean-clad, pony-tail wearing, hard-working electrician who worked alongside Heath in his construction business Monday to Friday. There was no way he could fail to notice the change, she'd told herself as she stared at her reflection in the bedroom mirror. There was no way he could look at her with all this girly, feminine enhancement and not recognize that she was a woman.

Hah. Showed what she knew. How willfuly deluded she was. How naive.

The moment she'd arrived in the ballroom, Andie had shed her coat and scanned the crowd, looking for Heath. When she hadn't found him, she'd positioned herself oh-so-casually near the entrance, arranging herself in the come-hither pose she'd practiced for a full hour in her mirror. Then he'd walked in, and her heart had gone absolutely nuts in her chest at the sight of him in black tie, the crisp white-ness of his shirt showing off his tan and making his dark chocolate eyes seem even darker. She'd forgotten all about her pose, raising a hand in a small, eager wave. She hadn't spared a glance for the woman trailing after him – there was always a woman trailing after him – and had forgotten to breathe when he spotted her and smiled. Everything south of her belly button had caught fire, and she'd waited for his eyes to go wide and for his gaze to make a slow, disbelieving, enlightening scan of her body as he saw her properly – really saw her – for the first time.

Instead, he'd crossed to her side and given her a friendly punch on the shoulder, exactly as her brother would have.

"Looking good, kid," he'd said. And then he'd intro-duced her to his date, and the two of them had disappeared into the crowd in search of their table.

He hadn't noticed the dress or the shoes or the hair. He hadn't been stunned by the beauty the Macy's girl had coaxed out of Andie's perfectly-acceptable-but-nothing-spectacular face. He just…hadn't. Because he didn't see her that way. She wasn't a woman to him. She was a sister. A workmate. A friend. Someone to go fishing with. Someone to grab a beer with. Not someone to hold close on the dance floor. Not someone to take home and press against a wall while he kissed her senseless and did amazing things to her body.

Andie gulped the last of the wine from her glass and looked around for more. There was half a bottle on the abandoned table to her right. Yanking her long skirt up so she wouldn't trip, she stood and leaned across to snag the bottle. She was going to feel like hell tomorrow, but right now she felt like crap, so what was the difference?

She was settling back into her chair when a woman dressed in black stopped at her table.

"Here," she said, thrusting a sheaf of papers stapled at one corner at Andie. "We're low on entries, so don't be shy. You never know, you might win. And if you're married already, pass it on to a friend, because the odds are really good with the entry numbers so low."

Andie shook her head, utterly bamboozled by every word that had come out of the other woman's mouth. Before she could ask for clarification, the woman in black was gone. Andie glanced at the papers. Be a Part of The Great Wedding Giveaway, the title proclaimed in bold font. Andie let out an involuntary bark of laughter. This night was getting better and better by the second.

Way to rub my face in the fact that I'm twenty-six years old, single, and in love with a man who will never look at me twice, Universe. Thanks a lot.

Morbid curiosity made her read further. The list of the prizes up for grabs was actually pretty impressive – the wedding dress, the groom's suit, flowers, the wedding reception. There was even a set of hand-crafted bedroom furniture for the lucky couple. As if they hadn't already hit the jackpot by meeting and falling love with each other in the first place.

The music changed to a smoochy Marvin Gaye song, and she glanced across at the dance floor. Heath was whispering in his date's ear, a naughty, suggestive smile on his lips. His date laughed, flicking her long hair over her shoulder in a way that should have made her look like a horse but instead looked sexy and confident and alluring.

Three things Andie would never be. Damn it.

She poured herself another glass of wine and brooded as she watched them slow dance. If this night had turned out the way she'd dreamed it, that would be *her* in Heath's arms right now. He'd be whispering in *her* ear, telling her all the sweet, dirty things he was going to do to her. She closed her eyes for a beat, imagining.

He'd drive her home, one hand on her thigh. Not too

high, but high enough that she'd know he meant business. He'd kiss her on the front porch, unable to wait until they were inside, his hands gliding down her back to cup her butt –

Her chair jerked, and she started, opening her eyes.

"So sorry, Ma'am," a waiter said before moving off.

Andie stared at the blank entry form in front of her. This night sucked so hard, she couldn't even enjoy a perfectly innocent fantasy without it being ruined. She blinked, aware that self-pitying tears weren't far away.

The only thing worse than sitting here on her own like a sad, needy loser would be sitting here crying into her wine glass.

Without really registering it, she read the first question on the form. *Describe how you and your fiancé first met.*

She'd been six years old and stuck up the apple tree in the backyard of her childhood home the day Beau brought Heath over to their place the first time. She'd dared herself to climb as high as she could, then frozen when she caught sight of the ground far, far below. She'd been stuck in the tree for nearly an hour when her brother came down to the bottom of the yard to introduce her to his new friend. Pride had forced Andie to pretend nothing was wrong, and pride had kept her hands steady when Heath and Beau climbed up to check out the view. Heath had looked at her with approval once they'd reached her branch, impressed with the height she'd achieved, and damn if she hadn't climbed down the trunk as confident as a monkey when they all decided they'd had enough.

Probably not the kind of cute-meet story the judging committee were looking for. They'd probably want something sentimental and meaningful. Or magically destined. Say, for example, if she and Heath had both been reaching for the last packet of white chocolate fudge at Copper Mountain Chocolates, and their hands had touched, and sparks had flown.

Andie reached for her small evening bag, pulling out a pen. It was stupid, and she was drunk, but she figured it wouldn't hurt to just jot down a few little details. A harmless self-indulgence where she pretended for a few precious minutes that the world was the way her heart wanted it to be.

She started writing, and the words poured from her pen. Thirteen years' worth of longing and yearning and fantasizing. She described the first date of her dreams. She outlined Heath's proposal, complete with him on his knee with a small velvet box. She wrote about why she loved him, describing how sweet and funny he could be, how hardworking and honest. She poured her heart onto the page, and the next time she became aware of the world again, the dance floor was almost empty and her hand was cramping from writing so much. She shook it out, a little dazed by how lost she'd become in a relationship that would only ever exist in her imagination – she'd filled out the whole form, all four pages of it, including the groom's section.

It was dumb, maybe even a little crazy, but she felt better for it. As though she'd gotten something off her chest.

"Still here?"

She glanced up into Heath's brown eyes, her heart jumping into her throat.

"Hey." She slid her forearm over the form, desperate to obscure it.

If he saw his name next to hers, if he read what she'd written... She'd have to leave town, change her name and never return. But not before imploding from humiliation.

"Where's your date?" Heath asked, dropping into the chair next to her. He'd pulled his tie loose and unbuttoned his shirt collar. With his dark curly hair tamed for the evening, he looked as though he should be on stage at Vegas, singing with Dean Martin and the other members of the Rat Pack.

"I, um, didn't come with anyone," she said. It was tempting to lie about having a date, but those kinds of fibs always came back to bite a girl on the ass, in her experience.

"Don't tell me you're on the prowl?" Heath said with a grin. "If your brother hears that, he'll be polishing his shotgun."

"Well, as you can see, it wasn't exactly a huge success," Andie said. "So he can relax. And you can keep your mouth shut."

His smile was warmly affectionate, his big body loose and relaxed. "As if I'd squeal on you, Panda."

Andie felt her smile falter at his use of her childhood nickname. "I really wish you wouldn't call me that."

"Can't help it. It's stuck in my brain, part of the architecture now."

"Then renovate and lose that room," she said. "I hate that nickname."

"It's cute.'"

"I'm not cute, in case you hadn't noticed. I'm nearly as tall as you."

"True."

His gaze wandered over her shoulder, looking for someone. Andie stared at the triangle of golden skin revealed by his open collar. How she wanted to press her face against that spot and simply inhale the good, hot smell of him. She curled her hands into fists, just in case they were tempted to go rogue on her.

"There she is. Gotta go. See you on Monday, Panda." Heath pushed to his feet, six foot one of solid, hard-earned muscle.

She opened her mouth to protest again, but then realized it was pointless. As this whole night had so brutally demonstrated, she would always be Beau Bennett's little sister to Heath, no matter what she did or said or wore. She shut her mouth with a click, and glanced down at her hands.

"Sorry, Andie."

The sincerity in his tone made her look up again.

"I'll try, okay? If you really hate it."

"I really hate it," she said.

"Then I'll do my best to change the record." He pulled his keys from his pocket. "You got a ride home?"

"All sorted, thanks."

Now, *that* was a lie, but she'd rather walk home in these torture shoes than sit in the back of Heath's SUV while Heath's brunette-of-the-moment sat up front with him.

"Then I'll catch you later." He bent down and pressed a kiss to her forehead, enveloping her for a few heady seconds in the scent of his woody, leathery aftershave. And then he was striding away from her, hooking an arm around his date's shoulders as they headed for the door.

She pressed her fingertips to her forehead, to the exact spot where he'd kissed her.

On her forehead.

As though she was a little kid.

Then she looked at the forms in front of her, the forms she'd just filled to overflowing with her childish fantasies.

You are a fool, Andie Bennett. Your own worst enemy. When are you going to let go of this stupid dream?

A terrible fury gripped her as the sheer unfairness of it all hit her. She loved Heath more than anything, and he had no idea, wasting himself on women who never seemed to stick. She would be a great partner for him, perfect. But he simply couldn't see it, and she had wasted years of her life wanting things to be different.

For a long, dangerous moment she was overwhelmed

with the need to smash something. Hell, she could tear up the whole ballroom, she was so angry.

And then, as quickly as it had hit her, the rage passed, leaving her with nothing but a churning, acid feeling in her gut and the certainty that if she didn't hustle, she was about to lose her dinner and many glasses of wine down the front of her very expensive gown.

One hand clapped to her mouth, she lifted her skirt with the other and surged to her feet. The few die-hards still lingering stepped out of the way as she charged for the door.

She barely made it to the ladies' room before the first spasm hit her, and she spent the next ten minutes reacquainting herself with the contents of her stomach.

Yep, this night was a real doozy.

But at least it was mostly over. There was that to be grateful for.

Chapter Two

Three months later

"COME ON, ANDIE. It's quitting time."

Heath's deep tones echoed up through the manhole into the roof space where Andie was working. She finished tightening the connection on the LED downlight she'd just installed, then tucked her screwdriver into her work belt.

"You are the worst boss in the world. I'm trying to get this finished, in case you hadn't noticed," she called back.

"It's Friday, and we're on time and on budget. Get your ass down here so I can buy you a beer."

"Five minutes," she promised.

She barely registered Heath's heavy tread as he headed for the door. She was too busy double checking her work one last time before grabbing the reel of cable she'd been working with. It was tempting to leave it in the roof space until she was on the job again Monday morning, but she'd seen too many residential developments raided by opportunistic kids and grifters over the years to risk it. Once, they'd returned to a worksite after Memorial Day weekend to discover the entire house had been stripped of its copper wiring and piping. As a result, her policy these days was always better to be safe than sorry.

She made her way to the manhole, moving nimbly from one roof beam to the next, then lowering herself to the ladder positioned underneath. She folded the ladder, and took both it and the reel of cable with her as she exited the house. She could see the rest of the crew gathered at the head of the cul-de-sac around the job trailer, and she made a quick detour by her pickup to dump her burdens before joining them. Big Mack and Angelo were tossing a football back and forth, while Pete, Rory and Mathew were sitting on the tailgate of Rory's battered pickup, all three of them already sucking down cold drinks.

Pete handed her an icy-cold root beer without her having to say a word when she joined them and she gave him a grateful smile.

"You're a good man," she said as she cracked the can open.

Resting her back against the sun-warmed metal of Rory's pickup, she gazed out at the ten homes in various stages of construction curving around the cul-de-sac. Every single one was a McGregor Construction home, and she couldn't help feeling a warm sense of pride on Heath's behalf. This was their biggest project yet, and there wasn't a doubt in her mind that the next would be bigger still. Heath might be quiet about it, but he was an ambitious man. One of the many things she admired about him.

"What you got planned for the weekend, Andie?" Rory asked, his head tilted back as he soaked up the rays.

"Bit of this and that. Thinking of going for a hike. Haven't decided yet," she said. "How about you?"

"Ella's 8th birthday." He shrugged.

"A houseful of screaming kids. You poor bastard," Mathew said.

"Hey, that's my princess you're talking about," Rory said.

"So you don't want to come fishing with me and Pete, then?" Mathew asked.

Rory looked pained. "Oh, man. Can't you wait until next week?"

Andie hid her smile behind the can of root beer, well aware that the guys were just winding Rory up. Sometimes it was easy to forget they were grown, adult men, they spent so much time ragging on each other.

Not that she didn't give and get her fair share of crap, too. She could more than hold her own when called upon. In fact, she prided herself on it. It was one of the many reasons she'd thrived in an industry that was almost one hundred percent male.

The sound of a car engine drew her gaze to the street and she watched as a small dark blue SUV pulled up just shy of where the guys were fooling around with the football. A slim, stylish woman with shoulder-length brown hair climbed out of the car and took a moment to get her bearings before striding toward them.

"If you're looking for Heath, he's in the trailer," Pete said helpfully.

"Thanks. I'm also looking for Andie Bennett."

All the little hairs on the back of Andie's neck stood on end as the other woman's gaze honed in on her.

"That's me," she said, shaking off the odd sensation as she pushed away from the pickup.

The woman smiled broadly. "I thought so. I'm Jane Weiss, Marietta Chamber of Commerce."

She offered her hand and Andie shook it bemusedly. What on earth did someone from the Chamber of Commerce want with her?

"I've got some incredibly exciting news for you and Heath, Andie. As you know, we announced the eight semi-finalist couples for Marietta's Great Wedding Giveaway a couple of weeks ago."

She paused, clearly waiting for Andie to respond, but since Andie hadn't exactly been slavishly following the coverage of the giveaway, all she could do was nod and continue to be baffled.

"It seems that one of our couples couldn't wait until August to get married, so we've had a couple drop out. And then we lost another couple because...well, their plans have changed." Jane pulled a face, which Andie guessed meant that the couple were no longer getting married. Awkward, having to back out of a competition as well as an engagement.

"Anyway, the Committee made a decision last night that with two drop-outs we should really give some of the runners-up a second chance. I'm sure you can guess where this is going." Jane's eyes were bright with anticipation.

"Um...Not really."

"You and Heath are now semi-finalists!"

Andie stared at the other woman. What craziness was this? "But –"

She blinked as a memory came back to her in a horrible rush – the woman handing out forms the night of the Valentine's Ball, the fantasy she'd poured onto the page in a fit of maudlin lunacy, having to rush off to the bathroom to lose her dinner...

Sweet Baby Cheeses, someone must have found her abandoned entry and handed it in.

Oh boy. Oh. Boy.

Oh boy oh boy oh boy.

There was a rushing sound in her ears. The ground seemed to shift beneath her feet. For the first time in her life she thought she might actually faint.

"Andie and Heath? You've got to be kidding." Pete's voice sounded as though it was coming from a long way away. "Talk about being punked."

The guys were all laughing. Jane was looking confused.

And then another voice chimed in, and Andie willed the earth to open up and swallow her.

"What's this about me and Andie?" Heath asked.

HEATH LOOKED FROM the woman in the neat suit to Andie. Who, he noted, was paler than he'd ever seen her before, her expression bordering on stricken.

Suit lady held out her hand for him to shake, a friendly smile on her lips. "Jane Weiss, Chamber of Commerce. I was just telling your fiancée–"

"Fiancée–?" Heath said.

"I was just telling Andie that you are now semi-finalists in the Great Wedding Giveaway."

Andie's gaze was glued to the ground, but she made a small, wordless sound of distress. The guys were all nudging each other, some of them smirking.

"You been holding out on us, boss?" Big Mack said before loosing a big belly laugh.

"Yeah, somebody has sure as hell messed up in there at Town Hall," Matthew said. "Andie and Heath. Can you believe it?"

Jane frowned, clearly trying to work out what was going on. "I'm a little confused. Did you and Andie enter the competition or not?"

Andie made another distressed sound, and instead of being pale her face was now beet red. He could practically feel the heat radiating off her cheeks. He waited for her to lift her gaze or say something, but she seemed paralyzed by whatever strong emotion had her in its grip.

"Sorry, Ms. Weiss, but would you mind giving Andie and me a second, please?" he said, not taking his gaze from Andie's face.

Grabbing Andie by the elbow, he steered her up the stairs to the job trailer. Shutting the door behind them, he turned to her.

"You want to tell me what's going on?" he asked quietly.

Andie lifted a shaking hand to her forehead, kneading the skin there, an old habit of hers since she was a kid.

"I have no idea how this happened."

"How what happened? Why on earth would this woman think you and I were getting married?"

Andie shook her head, her ponytail swishing across her shoulders. "I have no idea. I mean, I have *some* idea, but I still don't know how…"

She shot him an anguished look, and he could see she was mortified, about as embarrassed as he'd ever seen anyone be.

"Tell me the bit you do know."

"Okay. They were handing out forms at the Valentine's Day ball, for the wedding giveaway. The woman said they didn't have enough entries, and I didn't get a chance to tell her I wasn't interested. I was drunk enough that it seemed like a pretty funny idea to just fill it out to kill the time. I…I

19

stuck your name on it because it was the first one that popped into my head, and I made up a bunch of baloney. I can't even remember half of it…"

He shook his head. "You entered us in a wedding giveaway competition?" He couldn't quite get his head around it.

"No! No way. I didn't *enter* us. Only a mad person would do that. God, no. I just filled out the form. As a joke. But then I had to rush off to the bathroom because…well, because, and I forgot about the entry form. I guess someone must have found it and handed it in." Andie's face was still flushed, her expression pained. "I'm really sorry."

He studied her, trying to understand what was really going on, because something about her explanation didn't quite sit right with him. Then he flashed back to the night of the Valentine's Ball. He'd stopped by Andie's table before heading home, and now that he came to think about it, she'd been more than a little glassy-eyed.

His mouth twitched. "You must have written some pretty good baloney if we got picked as semi-finalists."

Now that he understood the mix-up, he couldn't stop himself from smiling. The idea of the two of them getting married was absurd. Beyond absurd, really. For starters, they would never have even started dating because Beau would have gutted him the second it looked as though Heath was going to lay a finger on his little sister. Then there was the fact that Andie worked for him…

"Please tell me you are not laughing at me," Andie said.

"You've got to admit, it's kind of funny."

"No, it isn't. People think we're engaged, Heath. There's a woman out there who thinks we're in the running for an all-expenses paid wedding." Her eyes were wide, her shoulders hunched up around her ears.

"Relax. We'll just explain what happened, and they can pick someone else."

"Oh, yeah, it's that easy," she said, throwing her hands in the air.

"No one is going to hold us at gunpoint and make us marry because you filled out an entry form when you were hammered, Andie."

"I'm not worried about the competition. I'm worried about *them*," she said, jabbing a finger toward the door.

It took him a second to understand she meant the crew.

"They are going to crucify me when they hear about this."

He opened his mouth to deny it, then thought better of it. Andie knew as well as he did what the guys were like. And she was right, they *were* relentless. Once they got wind of what had happened, they would rag on Andie for weeks. There would be running gags, new nicknames. Hell, he'd get his share of grief, too, no doubt.

"God. I'm such an idiot," she muttered, kneading her forehead again.

A knock drew him to the door, and he opened it to find Jane standing there, an envelope in hand.

"I'm so sorry, but I have another meeting I need to get to." Her gaze shifted over his shoulder to Andie and she lowered her voice. "I'm really sorry if I've created some kind of a problem here. It occurred to me just now that maybe you two were keeping your relationship on the down-low because of your work situation."

Heath took a deep breath, ready to wade in and start untangling the mess Andie's drunken joke had gotten them into. Then his gaze fell on the pack of very interested men gathered near the bottom of the trailer steps, their ears flapping shamelessly as they waited for the next installment in their own personal soap opera.

An image of Andie's beet-red face popped into his head.

"Don't worry about it," he said.

"You're sure? Andie looks a little shell-shocked."

Out of the corner of his eye, he saw Big Mack shift his weight expectantly.

"It's nothing that can't wait," he said.

"Great." Jane's smile was relieved. "Inside this envelope is everything you need to know about being semi-finalists, including contact details for the *Copper Mountain Courier* for a profile story they want to do on the two of you. My card is in there, too. If you have any questions, please don't hesitate to call me." Jane thrust the envelope into his hands. "And congratulations. I have to say, I was always a big fan of your entry. If you'd had a video like the other couples, you would have been a shoo-in for the first round."

She didn't give him a chance to respond, descending the steps and heading for her SUV.

"You got something you need to tell us, boss?" Angelo asked.

It was like feeding time at the zoo, the way they were all waiting for him to throw them something they could sink their teeth into.

"Yeah. Go home. Don't you know it's Friday?" he said.

He shut the door and turned back to Andie. She was frowning, her arms crossed tightly over her chest.

"Why didn't you tell her?"

"Because you're right, the guys would have a field day. I'll call her later and explain."

Andie closed her eyes for a long beat. "Please don't be nice to me right now, Heath. You should be kicking my ass."

"But then Beau would kick my ass, and I have a healthy survival instinct."

He slung his arm around her shoulders and gave her a squeeze, hoping to cajole the tight look off her face. She was so tense, it was like hugging a rock.

"Relax. We'll tell the guys it was an admin mix-up on Monday, and it'll die a natural death. Problem solved."

"I should be the one who calls the Chamber of Commerce lady and tells her the truth," Andie said. "I'm the one who made the mess. I should be the one who cleans it up."

"Okay, if that's what you want."

"It is." She wriggled out from beneath his arm. "I'm really sorry."

"Quit apologizing. We all make mistakes."

"When was the last time you made a mistake as ridiculous as this?"

He thought for a second. "Sharon?"

Andie huffed out a reluctant laugh. "Well, yeah, okay. She wasn't your best decision."

At least he'd gotten her to smile.

"Breaking up with her was."

"I'll give you that." Andie glanced toward the door. "I'm going to go. But I promise I'll clear things up over the weekend."

"I trust you, Andie."

She stared at him for a heartbeat, then shook her head. "Have a good weekend."

He watched as she exited the trailer, her long-legged stride slower than usual. This mix-up had obviously knocked her off kilter. He frowned as the niggling everything-is-not-as-it-appears-to-be feeling came back to him. Then he reminded himself that this was Andie.

She was one of the most level-headed, reliable, good-hearted people he knew. She honored her commitments, was as loyal as an old boot, and never shirked or made excuses. She was hands-down one of his best employees, if not *the* best, as well as being one of his best friends. She could out-fish him, came close to out-shooting him, and was as fearless as a damned teenager when they took his dirt bikes out for a run.

If she had something else going on, she'd lay it on the table. He was almost certain of it.

Still frowning, he locked up the trailer and went to do a last check on the site before hanging up his hat for the day.

Chapter Three

ANDIE WAITED UNTIL she was well away from the housing development before she pulled over and rested her forehead on the steering wheel. She felt as though she'd just gone ten rounds with Muhammed Ali – her McGregor Construction polo shirt was damp with sweat, and her legs were shaky. She was even a little breathless.

There were no words to describe how humiliated she felt right now – and the worst thing was, she'd brought it all on herself. Why on earth had she filled out that form the night of the Valentine's ball? And why on earth hadn't she torn it into nice, safe, tiny pieces once she was done?

Being drunk was no excuse. She'd put Heath in an incredibly embarrassing situation. A thousand other guys would be backing away from her at a million miles an hour right now, or at the very least giving her the side eye. But Heath believed her story, because he trusted her. And why wouldn't he? She was like his sister, he'd told her so often enough.

After a few minutes of trying to calm her swirling

thoughts, Andie lifted her head and let out a long breath.

The truth was, she'd gotten off lightly for what was a truly monumental mistake. All she had to do was tell the woman at the Chamber of Commerce that she and Heath were withdrawing from the competition and this would all go away.

It could have been a lot worse. There could have been an announcement in the paper, for example, and everyone in town might have found out about it. She shuddered, imagining how bad that would have been. Fortunately, however, the mess she'd created was containable, the damage limited. Heath was absolutely right when he said that the guys would forget about it over the weekend, and even if one or two of them remained curious, it would be easy enough to write it off as a clerical error or practical joke.

She let out another sigh, then reached for her phone, calling her neighbor, Lily, who also happened to be her best friend.

"I need copious quantities of alcohol and someone who won't judge me," she said when her friend picked up.

"I know just who to call," Lily said.

Andie smiled. Trust Lily to make her feel better right out of the gate.

"I can meet you at Grey's in twenty," Lily said.

"Done. I'll be the one in the corner, hiding my face in shame."

"I can probably make it in fifteen. Don't do anything

stupid before I get there."

"Too late."

"Then have a drink waiting for me. My day has also sucked big hairy ones."

Andie was still smiling as she ended the call. Growing up, she'd had a couple of close female friends, but both Joelle and Skylar had moved away for college and not come back. They tried to keep in contact with phone calls and Skype sessions, but there had been a profound vacuum in Andie's life until Lily moved into the apartment next to hers four years ago. She'd come over on the first night to ask for directions to the nearest bar, and they'd been fast friends ever since.

Thank God, because sometimes Lily's irreverent, mouthy take on the world was the only thing that kept Andie sane.

Being Friday, it was hard to find a parking spot near Grey's Saloon, but Andie got lucky when someone pulled out and she was soon walking into the crowded bar. She got even luckier when she spotted a couple exiting a booth in the back corner. Slipping through the crowd, she managed to get there before any other eagle-eyed patrons, offering up an apologetic smile to a couple of also-rans as she slid onto the bench seat.

"Andie Bennett. What can I do you for?" Reese Kendrick asked, leaning over to wipe down the table as he waited for her order.

"I'll have a beer and a pitcher of margaritas, thanks," Andie said. "And some spicy chicken wings. Oh, and some curly fries."

"Big day, huh?" he asked with an amused quirk of his eyebrow.

"You have no idea."

He flashed a smile at her before heading back to the bar. She stared after him, wondering why she couldn't have fallen for him, or one of the other eligible men who populated the town of Marietta. Anyone else, really, other than Heath McGregor. Reese was a good-looking guy. He'd even flirted with her one or two times. Granted, that had probably been professional flirting, the kind designed to get women to buy more drinks and leave good tips, but still, it had been flirting. And yet she didn't feel a thing when she looked into his eyes or when he smiled at her.

All Heath had to do was brush past her, or laugh at one of her jokes, or sling his arm around her shoulders, and she was gone. Her body on fire, her heart rate through the roof, every nerve ending screaming for more.

It wasn't fair. It truly wasn't, but it had been that way since she was thirteen years old. One day, Heath had simply been her brother's cool best friend, the one who taught her how to tie a six-turn San Diego jam and who always had time to talk with her, the next he was the sun, the moon and the stars. She didn't know how or why the transition had happened, it just had, and she'd never gotten over it or transferred her affections to someone else. And it wasn't as though she hadn't tried.

In her senior year of high school, she'd gone out with Jacob Paine for almost eight months. He'd liked her, she'd liked him, and it had been clear to her by then that Heath did not consider her a real woman or a romantic prospect in any way. So she'd settled. Jacob was fun, he looked good, he was into her. They dated, fooled around. The night of prom, she gave him her virginity, because it seemed like it was about time to be done with the damned thing and because she liked him a lot.

Jacob had naturally wanted to parlay that one night into more, but after a few weeks, Andie had known she couldn't continue to fool herself or him. Her heart was otherwise engaged, and even though she was as inexperienced as any other near-virgin, she'd known that she should probably feel something more than a little flushed and warm when she was naked with a man. She'd ended the relationship and Jacob had moved on while Andie remained stuck.

Her drinks arrived at the same time as Lily, who slid on-to the bench opposite in a wash of floral perfume.

"Perfect timing," Lily said, reaching for the pitcher of margaritas and pouring herself a huge drink. Flicking her straight dark hair back over her shoulder, she downed it in one big, long swallow.

"Wow. You weren't kidding about your day sucking, were you?" Andie said.

"I quit."

"Lily." Andie's smile dropped like a rock and she reached across the table to take her friend's hand. "What did he do?"

Because she knew it had to be something to do with Lily's sleazy, grabby boss. She'd been hearing stories about him for months now, and together they'd formulated strategies for her friend to avoid him, deflect him, repel him. Nothing had worked. And now, it seemed, things had come to a head.

"He tried to corner me in his office."

"And?"

"I kneed him so hard he may not be able to father children."

"That's okay, he already has three with his wife of twenty years," Andie pointed out dryly. "Are you okay?"

Lily pulled a face. "Sexual harassment isn't my favorite office past-time."

"You should sue him," Andie said.

"I should, but I'm not going to, because I don't have money for a lawyer." Lily sighed, her shoulders sinking lower. "And now I need to get my CV out there again. Damn it."

"Please let me talk to Beau about a job," Andie said.

She'd been trying to encourage Lily away from Mr. Grabby's employ for months now, offering to fix her up with her brother's security company. She was sure Beau would be able to find a position for Lily if Andie asked him to.

"No."

"Why not?"

"Because he doesn't like me, and I don't want to be in his debt," Lily said stubbornly.

"Beau doesn't not like you," Andie said. "He barely knows you."

"Come on, Andie. He doesn't like that I used to be a stripper. It's in his eyes every time he looks at me."

"I don't see that."

"That's because you're not looking hard enough. Anyway, enough about me. You were the one who lit the bat signal. Make me feel better about my sucky day by telling me about your sucky day."

Lily refilled her glass and folded her hands in front of her like a schoolkid waiting expectantly in class. Even though Andie wasn't finished with the topic of her brother helping Lily out, she very badly needed the balm of her friend's sympathy right now, so she launched into a retelling of her disastrous afternoon, carefully skirting around certain details to avoid incriminating herself.

Lily gasped in all the appropriate places like the good friend she was, her eyes wide with horror, and Andie was already feeling better by the time she was explaining how she'd left things with Heath.

"Okay. Your bad day officially tops my bad day," Lily said. "What a monumental screw-up. How on earth could the Chamber of Commerce get things so ass backwards?"

Andie downed the last of her beer. She'd been very vague

about the accidentally-entering-the-wedding-giveaway part of the story, hoping her friend would conveniently accept her sketchy version.

"That was my fault, actually. Remember the Valentine's Day ball? There was this woman handing out entry forms near the end of the night, desperate for more entries, and I was drunk. I looked up, Heath was the first person I saw, so I stuck his name on the entry form as a joke."

"But surely you had to do more than put someone's name down to be entered in the giveaway?" Lily looked perplexed.

"I made up some stuff. Like I said, I was plastered." She shrugged, hoping her friend would let the issue go.

But Lily's pansy-brown eyes remained steady on Andie for a long, long moment. So long that Andie had to fight the need to squirm in her seat.

"What's wrong? Do I have a beer moustache?" Andie asked, brushing her upper lip with her fingers.

"I'm trying to work out if I should let you get away with that sad ass story, or if I should call you on the fact that you have the world's biggest crush on Heath McGregor," Lily said.

Andie almost fell off the bench. "What? No. Where are you getting that from?" She was powerless to stop the color flooding into her face, however. "Heath is like my brother. *And* he's my boss. Did you take crazy pills today or something? I mean, me and Heath. Pfffft." Andie waved a hand as if batting away her friend's insane idea.

"Andie, I love you dearly, but you are not going to be in the running for an Academy Award any time soon," Lily said. "I've known how you feel about Heath for about two years now. Give or take. I've just been waiting for you to get around to admitting it to me."

Andie stared at her friend. "Two years? You've known for two years and you haven't said anything?"

"Hey, it's your deep, dark secret, not mine. We all have our skeletons in the closet, and I am a big respecter of skeletons."

Andie let her gaze drop to the table, feeling horribly exposed. There was a reason she'd never confessed her feelings to anyone else before. Then something occurred to her, and she lifted her gaze.

"It's not a crush," she said.

"Sweetie, you practically maul the man with your eyes when you think no one is looking."

"It's not a crush," Andie said stubbornly. If she was going to feel exposed, it might as well be for the truth. "I love him."

"Oh, Andie." Lily's voice was heavy with sadness. "I thought – I hoped – it was just a lust thing."

"No. I mean, it is, but it's more than that. It's lust *and* love. I want to jump him so much it hurts, but I want to spend the rest of my life with him, too." It was hard saying it, but Andie also felt a strange sense of relief and release.

She'd been sitting on these feelings for *years*.

Lily didn't respond immediately, instead pouring a decent slug of margarita mix into Andie's empty beer glass and pushing it toward Andie.

"What are you doing?" Andie asked.

"Preparing you." She reached across the table and caught both Andie's hands in hers. "What I am about to say may seem harsh and cruel, but I want you to know that it's said with so much love. So much."

"Okay," Andie said warily.

"All right, here we go. Brace yourself. If Heath were interested in you, he would have made a move by now. He sees you every day. You guys go camping together. He's had opportunities up the whazoo, Andie. And the man hasn't so much as glanced at you with carnal intent."

Andie waited for Lily to continue, but she appeared to be done.

"That's it?" Andie clarified.

"Yes."

"Oh, okay." Andie smiled, relieved.

"You're *smiling* after I just crushed your hopes and dreams?" Lily asked, incredulous.

"I know all that stuff. I've known it for years."

Lily looked baffled. "So...Wow, I'm really confused now. So if you're not holding out hope of Heath having a hallelujah moment, then why did you get all gussied up for the Valentine's Day ball?"

Andie narrowed her eyes. She'd begged Lily to come to the dance with her, but her friend had claimed the tickets were too expensive. Hence Andie being free to make a complete fool of herself that night without the intervention of a level-headed wingwoman.

"Is that why you wouldn't come to the ball with me?" Andie asked. "Because you didn't want to encourage me?"

"No. I didn't go because it was too damned expensive. But I knew why you were going. You were hoping for a *Pretty Woman* moment."

There was no point denying it – that was exactly what Andie had been hoping for. But that didn't mean she was deluded where Heath was concerned. She was in love with him, and a part of her still hoped every day that he might return her feelings – but that part was infinitesimally small. Microscopic, really. The rest of her – the overwhelming majority of her – knew it was futile, hopeless, pointless to love him.

"I know the score," Andie said slowly, trying to explain. "But every now and then – once every five years or so – I have a moment where hope overrides common sense and I do something stupid... And then I get things under control again and life goes on."

"Jesus, Andie, that is so freaking sad," Lily said, taking a slug from her glass and blinking rapidly.

"Don't cry for me, Lily, for God's sake. I'm not that pathetic."

"You're not pathetic at all. You're smart and funny and brave and hot. I would totally be all over you if I were a lesbian. Or if I had a penis. It just kills me that Heath can't see all that and that he has no idea what a freaking treasure he has sitting right under his nose."

"Oh." Now Andie was the one blinking, trying not to cry. "Thanks."

"You need to get past this, Andie."

"I know."

"We need to find some hot new guy for you to fall for. Someone who will blow Heath McGregor out of the water."

Andie nodded, but she could feel her forehead wrinkling. Heath was extremely hot, with his dark, curly hair and big hard body and deep chocolate eyes. It was going to take a seriously molten level of hotness to surpass him.

"I know, we've got our work cut out for us," Lily said, reading her mind as only a best friend can. "But it's doable. I know it is."

Andie was about to respond when a shadow fell over the table and she glanced up to see Sharon Martin standing there, hands on her hips, her pretty face contorted into a frown.

"Tell me it isn't true," Sharon said, her green eyes bright with strong emotion.

"Hi, Sharon. Long time no see," Andie said, shooting Lily a look. Not for nothing had they called Sharon 'The Nutbar' the whole three months Heath had been dating her last year. The woman couldn't order a cup of coffee without turning it into a three ring circus.

"Is it true, or not, Andie? Are you and Heath engaged or not?" Sharon demanded, her voice razor sharp and loud enough to carry.

Andie blinked, her stomach lurching with sudden alarm. "Wh-where did you hear that?"

"It's all over town, people saying that you two are semi-finalists in the wedding giveaway. But I figured it had to be a mistake, because there's no way on earth Heath McGregor would marry you when he wouldn't marry me."

Lily gasped at the other woman's rudeness. "You want to think for a moment about what you just said, Sharon?"

"I want answers, that's what I want. Are you pregnant, Andie? Is that how you trapped him into marriage? Don't you have any pride at all?"

Sharon was speaking so loudly, half the saloon could hear, and Andie could feel people turning to stare and listen. Cold adrenalin washed through her, and for a moment all she could do was stare at the other woman while her heart pounded thickly in her chest and warmth flooded into her face. Then Sharon's words really hit her and her temper kicked in, welcome and hot, and her chin came up.

"No, Sharon, I am not pregnant, not that that's any business of yours."

"Then you must have done something to Heath, held some kind of gun to his head, because there is no way he'd asked someone like you to marry him when he could have had me."

Lily gasped again, and out of the corner of her eye Andie saw her friend move.

"I've got this," Andie told her.

She slid to the end of the booth and stood, making sure that Sharon had plenty of time to register the fact that Andie had a good eight inches on her.

"You know nothing about Heath McGregor, Sharon, and you know nothing about me, so why don't you quit making a fool of yourself and get out of my face?" Andie said.

Someone hooted their approval of her fighting words, but Andie didn't take her eyes from Sharon's.

"You really think you're woman enough to hold onto a man like him? I give it two months, tops," Sharon said contemptuously.

Andie smiled slowly, insulted and furious in equal measures. How dare Sharon stand there and impugn Andie's womanhood for all of Grey's to hear? How dare she suggest that Andie was less-than, some kind of feeble, pathetic consolation prize?

This bitch was going down.

"Not woman enough? That's not what Heath said last night in the car. And this morning in the shower. And the other day on the kitchen table. And it's definitely not what he's going to say tonight. You want to know what he does say, Sharon? *That he can't get enough.* Ever."

For the first time Sharon looked uncertain, and Andie felt a surge of triumph.

Then she glanced over the other woman's shoulder and realized the bar was as quiet as a church, every eye and ear attuned to the war of words. Her gaze went from face to face, recognizing friends, neighbors, men who worked for her brother, sisters of her work colleagues…

Holy crap.

Talk about putting your foot in it.

Her gaze found a too-familiar face at the bar, and her heart stopped. Heath stared back at her, his expression utterly unreadable, and time seemed to stand still as she understood that she was five seconds away from becoming the laughing stock of Marietta, Montana.

Her stomach clenched painfully as Heath pushed away from the bar. The crowd seemed to part as he walked slowly, deliberately toward her.

Oh, God. Why did I let my temper get away from me? Why did I have to say all those things? And why did he have to be here to hear them?

Andie stared at him, unable to look away as he came to a halt in front of her.

This was it. The moment where he opened his mouth and corrected the record and everyone knew that she was an idiot, a fantasist, a fraud.

She closed her eyes, waiting for the words that would seal her fate. A warm weight – his hand – landed on her shoulder. She opened her eyes just in time to see Heath lower his face toward her. Then he was kissing her, his arms sliding around her as he pulled her against his chest.

Her brain went off-line, completely blown away, but her body knew what to do. Her mouth opened beneath his, her hands finding his shoulders, one sliding up to palm the nape of his neck. Heat washed over her as his mouth moved over hers, commanding, demanding. She pressed closer still as she found his tongue with her own, stroking it boldly. She felt his shock, the ripple of it racing through his body, and then his tongue was in her mouth, stroking hers, and her hips were tight against his as his hand slid down to cup her butt and pull her more fully against him.

Someone cleared their throat. Heath's mouth stilled on hers, then he lifted his head. For a moment she stared into his eyes, utterly stunned, so turned on that parts of her body literally *ached* with need.

"So, Sharon, any more questions? Or are you done being a desperate psycho?" Lily said from somewhere behind her.

Andie blinked, crashing back to reality. Sharon, Grey's Saloon, Lily standing not three feet away, the whole town watching...

"You lied to me," Sharon said, stabbing a finger at Heath. "You told me you never wanted to marry."

"You must have misunderstood me," Heath said in a slow, easy drawl, his arm warm and heavy around Andie's shoulders now. "I meant I never wanted to marry you."

Andie was human enough that she enjoyed the way Sharon flinched away from his words. The other woman seemed at a loss as to how to respond to his verbal slap down, and after a few loaded seconds she settled for spinning on her heel and marching for the door.

"And good riddance," Lily muttered. "What a nut job."

"You okay?" Heath asked, and Andie could see the concern in his eyes when she forced herself to look into his face.

"Yes. Of course."

"Good. Want to get some air with me?"

"Um, sure."

Lily handed Andie her phone and wallet. "Call me when you get home. If you get home." Then she winked.

Andie could only stare at her. This was not a wink-worthy situation. She'd let her temper get the better of her and dug a huge hole for Heath and herself, and he'd once again come riding to her rescue, like the good guy he was – and then she'd taken advantage of his gallant gesture by sticking her tongue down his throat.

Not her finest hour, by a long shot.

Heath steered her toward the door, and she did her best to look as though she didn't have a care in the world, very aware of all the curious eyes on them. Heath opened the door for her, and she ducked her head as she brushed past him. The night air was warm for May, and Andie looked up and down the street before shoving her hands deep into the pockets of her Dickies work pants and turning to face the music.

Chapter Four

HEATH SUCKED IN some much needed fresh air, struggling to get his scrambled thoughts in order before he and Andie had the conversation they needed to have. Problem was, it was hard to think when he could still feel the press of her long, lean body against his.

She'd tasted liked strawberries. And beer. If anybody had ever told him that those two things would make a killer combination, he'd have laughed in their face.

He cleared his throat. "Sorry about that. I couldn't think of any other way to shut her up."

Andie blinked. "You're apologizing to me?"

"Sharon is my mistake. You shouldn't have to deal with the blow-back."

"I'm the one who got us into this whole mess in the first place. Remember?"

"No sane person would have made a public spectacle the way Sharon did just because they heard you and I were supposedly engaged. That part of the mess is mine."

"But if I hadn't let her get to me and said all those

things, you wouldn't have had to step in and...you know." She gestured vaguely with one hand, her gaze sliding away from his. "And now the whole town thinks you and I have got something going on. That is definitely all on me."

Heath couldn't help it; he could feel himself starting to smile.

"You had better not be laughing at me again," Andie said.

"We're standing out the front of Grey's arguing over who's the most responsible for a situation straight out of a slapstick movie. It's a little bit funny."

Andie didn't smile, though. "You heard the bit where the whole town thinks we've got something going on, right?"

"They'll realize they're wrong pretty quickly."

"Yes, they will, and Sharon will have a field day and a half," she said, her tone grim.

"I'll have a word with her," he said.

"Be serious. There is nothing you can say to her that will stop her from going to town on this situation," Andie said. "Unless —" She broke off and shook her head before finishing her thought.

"Unless what?"

She glanced at him quickly before returning her gaze to her work boots. "Nothing."

Heath studied her downturned head. The street light caught the tiny strands of hair that had escaped her ponytail, making them glow. She'd always been on the shy side, never one to put herself forward, which made the way she'd stood up to Sharon and pushed back even more notable. He could still hear her voice, clear as a bell, as she stared Sharon down. *That's not what Heath said last night in the car. And this morning in the shower. And the other day on the kitchen table. And it's definitely not what he's going to say tonight. You want to know what he does say, Sharon? That he can't get enough. Ever.*

He didn't blame her for fighting back – hell, if Sharon had been a man and Heath had been in Andie's shoes, Sharon would have been looking for her teeth right about now. The thing was, Andie's fighting words pretty much confirmed the rumor that they were engaged, which meant that any correction to the record would make her look like a liar at best. And Andie was right, Sharon was malicious enough to make a huge deal out of it once the truth was revealed, and Marietta's town gossips would finish the job.

Andie would be humiliated, and he knew her well enough to know that it would be something that stayed with her a long time. Witness her deer-in-the-car-headlights response when Jane Weiss had turned up at the worksite today. Andie was tough – she had to be, to thrive in a male-dominated workplace – but that didn't mean she wasn't sensitive. Her feelings ran deep, even if she didn't wear them on her sleeve.

"What if we didn't set the record straight right away?" he asked.

That brought her head up. "You mean, pretend we're

actually engaged?"

"That's what you were going to say before, right?"

"Yeah, but I didn't, because it's *insane.*"

"Sure, but this whole situation is straight up ridiculous."

Andie stared at him as though she was wondering if he'd sustained a head injury recently. "You clearly haven't thought this through. What about my brother?"

"We let him in on the secret."

"The guys at work?"

"It'll give them something to talk about."

"They'll want to know why we never said anything before."

"We'll tell them we didn't want things to change at work."

She glanced up the street, a frown on her face. He waited patiently as she thought it through.

"How long would we have to pretend for?" she asked.

"I don't know. When does this competition end?"

"I have no idea. It hasn't exactly been on my radar."

"So we find out, and we stay engaged until the winners are announced. And then we just quietly fade into the background and break up."

Andie shook her head. "It's nuts."

"The only other option is the truth."

She crossed her arms over her chest, worrying her lower lip with her teeth, obviously thinking through what that would look like. Finally she looked at him. "You're only doing this because I stuffed up hugely and you feel sorry for me."

"Yep. And because you're my friend and what Sharon said to you was way out of line."

Andie shrugged a dismissive shoulder, a frown on her face. "I shouldn't have bitten. If I'd just kept my mouth shut..."

But she hadn't. He waited as she paced away a few steps, then walked back.

"Okay. All right. I will take you up on your pity offer, because apparently I am a weeny who is more worried about what people think than I should be."

"You're human. And this is a small town."

She rolled her eyes, and he couldn't stop himself from reaching out and pulling her close for a hug. "It's not a big deal," he said.

He realized the moment he felt her body against his that hugging her so soon after the kiss was a mistake. All of a sudden he was remembering the way she'd melted into his arms, the feel of her small, firm backside in his hand, the sweet brush of her tongue in his mouth.

She was tense, too, and they broke apart after a second, neither of them making eye contact. Andie took a step backward, hands slipping into the back pockets of her khakis.

"I've got some stuff to do tonight, but we should probably work out some details over the weekend," she said.

"I'll call you."

"Okay." She nodded, then licked her lower lip nervously. "Well. Speak to you then."

She turned on her heel and took off, her stride long and brisk, her ponytail swinging against her back. His gaze dropped to her ass, but her khakis were too baggy to do justice to her neat little butt. Then he realized what he was doing, where his thoughts had gone, and shook his head.

That kind of crap stopped *right now*. Andie was his friend. Period. The fact that he now knew that she tasted like strawberries and kissed like a freaking dream had nothing to do with anything.

Shoulders tense, he headed back into Grey's for some much needed hard liquor.

ANDIE WANTED TO go home and crawl beneath the covers and pretend the last few hours of her life were a horrible nightmare she would soon wake up from, but she needed to talk to her brother. If he heard on the town grapevine that she and Heath were engaged, it wouldn't be pretty or quiet.

Teeth gritted, she headed out of town toward her brother's property, five acres of prime Montana land that fronted onto the Yellowstone river. The lights were on in the modest cabin that her brother called home, and she parked next to his black Ford Explorer. She didn't immediately get out of the car, drumming her hands on the steering wheel as she stared at the lit windows.

The thing with Beau was that he took the big brother thing very seriously. There were reasons for that, and she understood that his protectiveness came out of great love and the sense of responsibility he felt for her, but that didn't make it any easier being his sister sometimes.

For example, the day she'd moved into her apartment, he'd shown up with his tool kit and a bunch of window locks and insisted on installing them, even though she was on the third floor and the only way for someone to access her windows was to abseil down from the roof.

Every year he appeared the day after the first snow and commandeered her car, bringing it back an hour later with snow tires fitted, and she still cringed when she thought about the hour-long interview poor Jacob had had to sit through when he wanted to date her in senior year.

The front door opened, and a tall, dark figure filled the frame. Andie pulled the keys from the ignition.

"Thought it was you," Beau said as she mounted the front steps.

"You thought right."

Her brother's dark grey eyes scanned her face briefly. "What's wrong?"

"Why does anything have to be wrong?" she said.

"Because you look skittish, and you always look skittish when you've got a bug up your butt."

Andie gave him a look, but he simply shrugged.

"Just calling it like I see it."

She stood on tip toes and kissed his cheek. At six foot three, he was one of the few men she had to look up to.

"Why aren't you out partying hearty? It's Friday night," she said.

"When was the last time you saw me party?" Beau asked, shutting the door and leading her to the kitchen.

"Good point." She slid onto a stool at the counter and watching as he pulled down two mugs.

Her brother had a serious thing for coffee, something he'd picked up during his time in the Middle East. The shiny espresso machine on his kitchen bench was the newest thing in the house, and she watched with amusement as he fussed over grinding the beans.

"For all you know, I might not actually want a coffee," she said dryly.

He shot her a sideways glance from beneath his dark brows. "Seriously?"

"No. You know I love your coffee. But you shouldn't just assume that everyone is like you, juiced up on caffeine twenty-four-seven." She eyed his too-long hair and wrinkled clothes. "What time did you start this morning, anyway?"

"I don't know. Four? Five?"

Andie frowned at him. "You need to take care of yourself or you're going to burn out."

Two years ago, her brother had started up a private security company, quickly garnering contracts with several big retailers, local industrial operators and the Marietta school district. Andie had hoped he'd pull back from the punishing hours he'd been working during the start-up phase now that the business was running smoothly, but he showed no signs of easing up on himself.

"I can sleep when I'm dead."

"Tired people make mistakes," Andie said. It was something she'd had drummed into her during her apprenticeship, and she'd seen it happen on building sites over and over again. She hated the idea of her brother driving home late at night in an exhausted state.

Beau's mouth curled up at the corner. Folding his arms across his chest, he leaned against the counter. "You want to tell me what's going on, or do you want to keep trying to distract and divert me?"

Andie widened her eyes with outrage. "That was concern for someone I love, not a diversionary tactic."

"Okay, concern noted. Why are *you* here on a Friday night when you could be out partying?"

She reached up and pulled her hair free of its ponytail, massaging the back of her skull as her hair fell free. "I screwed up, big time," she said heavily.

It took her ten minutes to fill her brother in and answer all his questions, at the end of which he took a long pull from his coffee and eyed her steadily.

"So you and Heath are engaged."

"Fake engaged. Yes." Unlike Lily, she knew she didn't

have to worry that Beau might read more into the situation. Romance wasn't exactly his forte.

Beau shook his head, his mouth curling at the corner again. Andie slapped both palms onto the counter in exasperation.

"Don't tell me you think this is funny, too?" she demanded. "Why do the men in my life find my imminent humiliation so amusing?"

"Hell, yeah, I think it's funny. Heath is certifiable for getting sucked into any of this."

"He's saving my ass," Andie pointed out. "You should be thanking him."

"Just as long as he doesn't get carried away with the whole fiancé thing, I will."

"Trust me, that is not going to be a problem," Andie muttered, pushing her empty coffee cup away from herself.

Beau shot her a sharp look. "Should you be sounding disappointed about that?"

"I'm not."

"Heath is not the kind of guy you want to go out with, Andie," he said, suddenly very serious.

She breathed out through her teeth. "I'm twenty-six years old, Beau. I think I can decide the kind of men I want to go out with."

"Heath will not be one of them."

"Relax, okay? He's my boss. He's your friend. He's the last guy I'd want to be with," she lied shamelessly. No good would come of her brother guessing her secret. The thought alone made her shudder.

"Good, because he's not for you."

"Why? What's wrong with him? Has he got three penises? Does he turn into a wolf on a full moon? Is he going to handcuff me to his bed and spank me?"

Beau's mouth thinned. "Let's make a deal. You never say the word penis around me again, and I will scrub what you just said from my mind."

"Penis penis penis."

"Andie."

She pointed at her own chest. "Twenty-six years old. And not a virgin, okay?"

Beau's left eye got a little twitchy. "That's another word I don't want to hear again."

"You are ridiculous. I know about your women. Why is it you can do whatever you like and I have to be protected like some precious snowflake? And think carefully before you answer that question because if the words 'because you're a girl' are a part of it, you're in big trouble."

"You're my little sister."

"Dangerously close."

"I know the way guys think, Andie."

"News flash, Beau – girls think like that sometimes, too. Who cares as long as it's safe and consensual?"

Beau threw his hands in the air. "That's it, I'm out. I cannot have this conversation with you."

"I'm an adult. Deal with it."

"And yet you've somehow managed to get yourself fake engaged to my oldest friend."

Andie opened her mouth to retaliate, then realized she really didn't have much to say in her own defense. "True, I'm an idiot. But that doesn't mean I am not allowed to have a sex life, if I so choose."

Beau stuck his fingers in his ears. "Mary had a little lamb."

Andie laughed. He might be an overbearing, overprotective ass, but her brother was one of her favorite people in all the world, and she was one of the few people he allowed himself to be goofy with.

"I'm going home now," she said, "but if anyone asks, you're proud as punch that your baby sister is marrying your best friend. Got it? And the reason we didn't blab it all around town was because we work together and didn't want to mess with the dynamic."

"You're asking me to lie for you?"

"Yep, I am. And I want you to be convincing, too, because otherwise I'll have to leave town and have plastic surgery to hide my identity."

Beau followed her to the front door. "You should have taken Sharon out the back and tried a little non-verbal communication with her. Would have saved everyone a lot of trouble."

"I'll remember that next time I'm publicly insulted by a

deranged woman."

Beau caught her shoulder before she could start down the porch stairs. "Before you go. Dad called today. He and Trudy are going to be in town in September."

"How long are they staying?"

"Just for the weekend, I think. Trudy's got a show in Seattle."

Their father had married a successful artist after their parents' divorce when she was sixteen, and his life had pretty much been subsumed by hers from day one.

She nodded. "I'll mark it on my calendar."

She punched her brother on the arm and started down the steps.

"That hurt," Beau called after her.

"It should. You taught me how to punch," she said over her shoulder.

She'd left her phone in the pickup, and she grabbed it when she got in and added her father's visit to her calendar. She hadn't seen him face-to-face for nearly two years. Once, that would have made her incredibly sad, but she was resigned to his benign neglect these days. After Ben had died, he'd slowly drifted away from the rest of them. At the time, it had been baffling and hurtful and had destroyed their already-fragile family, but now Andie understood that he'd simply been doing what he needed to do to survive his grief.

No one was perfect, after all. Least of all her, and she had a drunken entry in a wedding giveaway competition to prove it.

The full impact of the day's events hit her then, sucker-punching her in the gut. Heath had saved her bacon tonight, and he was about to do it repeatedly for weeks on end as her pretend fiancé. A bubble of hysterical laughter rose up her throat as it occurred to her what she'd inadvertently done: signed up for her own personal version of Hell.

For as many weeks as it took, she would have to hold Heath's hand and let him put his arm around her and pretend that she was his and he was hers. And none of it would be real, even though her stupid heart longed for it to be so.

And there's no one to blame but yourself, dufus.

Always a comforting thought.

Fastening her seatbelt, she started her pickup and headed for home.

Chapter Five

THE PHONE'S BELLIGERENT, persistent ring dragged Andie out of sleep the next morning. Eyes squinted, she fumbled around on her bedside table until she found it.

Lily had insisted on dissecting every second of the scene in Grey's Saloon over and over with her when she got home, and it had been late when she finally said goodbye to her friend and hit the sack. She groaned when she saw the time on the phone – seven thirty – and hit the button to take the call.

"I was just about to hang up. Don't tell me you're still in bed?"

Heath's deep voice filled her ear and Andie's eyes popped all the way open.

"It's Saturday. My one sleep-in day."

"Which explains why you sound like a two-pack-a-day smoker."

"I haven't used my voice yet. Because I was asleep. Note the past tense."

"I told you I'd call."

"You didn't say it would be at the crack of dawn."

"Dawn was hours ago. I know, because I saw the sun come up."

"Now you're just bragging." Andie snuggled further beneath the covers. Having Heath in her bed – even virtually – was a rare pleasure, and she wasn't above enjoying it.

When you'd been nursing unrequited love for a man for years, you learned to take your moments where you could find them.

"Why were you up in time to see the sun rise?" she asked.

"I went for a run."

"You couldn't have done that at a civilized hour?"

"I had a bit on my mind."

Some of her lazy enjoyment faded away. Right. This was a business call. Sort of.

"If you're having second thoughts, I totally understand–"

"I'm not having second thoughts. I read through the information Jane left for us. It's pretty straight forward. They're announcing the winners at the Summer Solstice picnic in town. So we've got five weeks of being in the spotlight, then it's all over."

"Five weeks. Okay. I guess that's doable."

"The *Copper Mountain Courier* want to do a profile piece on us, but we can put them off. There's no need to turn this into a spectacle."

"God, no."

Although they were already halfway there.

"I figure we just keep our heads down, and this will all go away," he said.

"Good plan."

"All right. I'll let you go back to sleep."

She blinked. That was it?

"I thought we were going to work out the details."

"We just did."

She rolled her eyes. How like a man was that?

"Heath, people are going to want to know how long we've been together. They're going to ask how you proposed, and when we were planning on getting married... This is Marietta. They're going to be nosy."

Silence from his end of the phone. Then: "I hadn't thought about that."

"What are you doing for the rest of the day?" she asked.

Her heart gave a treacherous leap at the thought of spending time alone with Heath without the rest of the crew hanging around.

"I'm doing some work at the house," Heath said.

"I could come over and help and we could hash something out."

"You've done enough already."

Heath had been building his own home on the weekends and in-between jobs for the past twelve months. Andie and the rest of the crew had all helped out, but Heath had been very careful not to abuse their generosity.

"Consider it payment in kind for the five weeks you're about to spend pretending to be my fiancé," she said.

"When you put it that way…What time should I expect you?"

Andie glanced at the time. "Ten?"

"You're going back to sleep again, aren't you?"

"I am."

His laugh came down the line, warm and deep. She squeezed her thighs together. God, she loved his laugh. Almost as much as she loved his big, strong hands. And his eyes –

"Andie?"

"Sorry, did you say something?"

"I told you to wear old clothes. We'll be painting."

She groaned. She hated painting. "You could have told me that before I offered to help."

"But then you might not have offered."

"That's kind of the point."

He laughed again, and she curled her toes into the mattress.

"I'll see you at ten," he said.

"You will. I'm almost certain of it."

She ended the call and let her hand flop down onto the mattress, phone and all. Staring up at the ceiling, she let herself remember those few precious seconds from last night again. She'd been trying not to dwell on them, scared of wearing them out and sucking all the goodness from them, but her willpower was low after Heath's call.

She closed her eyes, going back to last night, remembering the way he'd rested his hand on her shoulder and turned her body ever so slightly toward him. The way his mouth had found hers so confidently. The knowing stroke of his tongue in her mouth. The feel of his hard chest against her breasts. The slide of his hand down her back, and the heat of his hand as he'd cupped her butt and pulled her more urgently against him...

She pressed a hand to her sternum. Her heart was going a mile a minute, her breath coming in short, sharp pants.

That kiss wasn't real. It was for show. You need to remember that.

She did. She so did. And she needed to remember that the only reason any of this was happening was because Heath felt sorry for her, because when all of this silliness was over, she still had to work for him and live in this town and be a part of his life.

She rolled onto her belly, determined to lull herself back to sleep. Fifteen minutes later, she gave up, throwing the covers back. She spent the next few hours tidying her apartment and catching up on laundry before showering and dressing in a pair of old jeans she'd hacked off at the knee and one of her brother's old shirts. She braided her hair before coiling it into a bun high on the back of her head, then gave herself a quick once over.

She looked like a tall, skinny boy with a girl's hairdo. But what was new about that?

Turning her back on the mirror, she grabbed her things and headed for the door. She made a quick stop at the bakery on the way out of town, then aimed her car northwest. Like her brother, Heath had bought himself a handful of acres just out of town, but his land was over near Riverbend Park on a rise that offered him a spectacular view of the town and the Absaroka Range. He'd designed the house himself to take full advantage of the views, and as always she got a funny tight feeling in her chest when she drove around the final bend in the road and saw it in all its glory.

Built from local stone and timber, it had an aggressive, jutting roofline that looked as though it was going to take flight, and huge expanses of glass to soak in the views. It was edgy and beautiful and clever, a testament to his vision and skill as a builder.

Last time she'd been here, she'd spent the day crawling around in the roof space installing the two enormous iron chandeliers Heath had chosen for the dining room as well as doing final fixes on the various power outlets and light switches throughout the house. That had been over a month ago, and she was keen to see how far Heath had progressed since then.

Collecting the bag of goodies from the bakery, she made her way over the churned-up earth to the stone-flagged entranceway. The double doors were huge and she had the unfamiliar sensation of actually feeling petite as she knocked and waited for Heath to answer.

The door swung open almost immediately, and she forgot what she was going to say, every thought blown away by the sight of Heath in ragged, worn jeans and an over-sized tank top that offered glimpses of his chest and torso. In case that wasn't enough, his face was dark with stubble, and his feet bare.

In short, he looked good enough to pounce on, push to the floor and ravish.

If you were that kind of girl.

Andie settled for swallowing the huge lump of lust in her throat and trying to appear normal.

"Hey," she said, lifting the bag of Danishes. "I bought sustenance."

"You're a mind reader. I was just about to start gnawing my arm off," Heath said, flashing her a smile.

Andie told herself not to swoon and glanced past him into the vast entrance hall. "How are things looking in there these days?"

"Come see."

He stepped aside so she could enter, and she saw that the entrance hall had already received a couple of coats of paint in a warm linen color. The walnut floorboards had yet to be polished – Heath wouldn't do that until after he'd finished painting – but she could already see how spectacular this space was going to be.

"Wow," she said.

Heath glanced around. "Yeah. It's coming up well."

"Says the master of the understatement. It's beautiful, Heath."

His smile was endearingly sweet. "Thanks."

He led her into the main living area, and she stopped in her tracks. The rustic wood mantlepiece above the enormous open fire was a new addition, along with the kickboards and other trims. Here the walls were a soft cafe latte, a color she wanted to reach out and touch, and she could only stand and shake her head at how stunning it all was.

"You are never going to want to leave this place," she said. "'We'll have to come pry you out of the house every morning with a crowbar to get you to the worksite."

Heath glanced around, and she could see the quiet pride in his face. She was well aware that as a teenager Heath had slept on a fold-out couch in his father's one-bedroom apartment for several years after his mother had taken off with a rodeo cowboy. You didn't need to be Dr. Freud to understand why he craved space, and why he'd put so much time, effort and imagination into creating a home that was all his own.

"Still not sure how I'm going to furnish this place, but I guess I'll work it out," Heath said.

Andie cocked her head, considering the room. "I think you should get a big sectional so you can make the most of the fireplace," she said. "And one of those patchwork rugs made up of sections from vintage Turkish rugs."

Heath squinted his eyes, as though trying to see her vision. "That could work."

"And you need good curtains and cushions. I know you men don't 'get them', but they make a difference."

"I'll take your word for it." Heath's gaze fell to the bag in her hand. "Can I have a Danish now?"

She tossed the bag at him. "Surprised you waited this long to ask."

He was already peering inside, his eyes bright with greed. "You got apple."

Of course she had. It was his favorite.

"They were still warm from the oven when I picked them up," she said.

Heath made a lip-smacking sound and she laughed.

"Come on. I've got some coffee in the kitchen," he said, gesturing with his chin.

He turned and headed through the wide doorway to his right, and she snuck a glance at his body before following him. The things he did for worn denim... The man should come with a hazard warning tied around his neck. And a bucket of cold water for women to douse themselves with.

He was pouring two cups of coffee when she entered, and he slid one across the cloth-covered counter toward her. Underneath the cloth, she knew, were wide counters crafted from gorgeous Crema Nuova marble, but Heath was carefully protecting them until the house was complete. Likewise, he hadn't installed the doors, drawers and kick plates yet, leaving the kitchen's bare carcass exposed for now.

"So. We need a story," Heath said as he tore the bakery bag in two, exposing the pastries.

Andie rubbed her hands down the thighs of her cut-offs. "Yeah. I think we should keep it simple. Something we can both remember. Something that people will believe."

Heath nodded, busy chewing on a Danish. She took a sip of coffee and was unable to stop herself from checking out the parts of his chest left exposed by the loose, low neckline of his tank top. Crisp dark hair covered his pecs – just enough to scream 'masculine' without getting into monkey costume territory – and she had a sudden, powerful sense memory of just how hot and hard all that muscle had felt when he'd yanked her up against him last night.

Her coffee went down the wrong way, and she nearly choked as she fought to get air and clear her throat at the same time.

"You okay?" Heath asked, concern on his face.

"Fine," she rasped. "Just swallowed the wrong way."

"Think you'd have the hang of that after twenty-six years," he said, gentle laughter in his eyes.

"Seems like it, but apparently I'm a slow learner," she said.

She took another mouthful of coffee, and this time it went down the right way. Mostly because she kept her gaze fixed firmly on Heath's face.

"So. A simple story," he said, his gaze becoming thoughtful. "I guess I asked you to marry me and you said yes isn't going to cut it?"

"People are going to want to know why you asked me. We've known each other half our lives. Why get together now?" Andie said.

Heath frowned, and Andie felt a stab of pain somewhere in the region of her heart. Was it really that hard for him to imagine why he might see her as something other than his oldest friend's little sister?

"What if I started seeing some new guy you didn't like, and you got jealous?" Andie suggested.

"I don't really do jealousy," Heath said.

Of course he didn't. He'd had his choice of women since the day his voice broke. What reason was there to be jealous of one particular woman when the queue of hopefuls formed to the left?

"Do you have a better idea?" Andie asked.

Heath's dark gaze raked her face and she could practically hear his brain ticking over. "What if something happened on the worksite, and it got me thinking? Maybe you nearly fell down a ladder and I caught you. Something like that."

Andie made a rude noise.

"I take it you don't approve?" he said.

"Can't we come up with a scenario where I don't have to be incompetent in order for you to be romantically attracted to me?"

Heath frowned. "I don't need for you to be incompetent

to be attracted to you."

A little thrill went through her at his words. She gave herself a mental slap.

He's not saying he's attracted to you, dufus. He's talking generally.

"How about this?" she said. "We had too much to drink one Friday after work, and you drove me home and something happened. We thought it was a one-off, but it turned out it wasn't, and we decided to keep our relationship on the down-low until we worked out what it was. Which is why the guys at work had no idea."

Heath nodded slowly. "Okay. That'll probably work. What about the proposal?"

"You were inspired by all the wedding competition talk, so you asked, and I said yes, and we entered on the night of the Valentine's Day ball on impulse, because they were low on entries, and never thought we'd stand a chance of winning."

"Well, that part at least has the virtue of being partly true," he said dryly.

"We'll just have to hope that no one remembers you were at the ball with someone else."

"Right. I'd forgotten about that."

Andie spared a thought for the brunette who'd been his date for the ball. No doubt she'd gotten all gussied up for the night in the hope that whatever was going on between her and Heath would turn into something real and permanent.

Little did she know that Heath didn't do either of the above.

"Did you mean what you said to Sharon?" Andie asked suddenly, unable to stop herself.

"That I didn't want to marry her? You seriously need to ask me that?" he asked, giving her a look as he reached for a second pastry.

"That you don't ever want to get married. Full stop." Andie glanced around the unfinished kitchen. This house boasted four bedrooms and three living areas. That was a lot of space for one man to rattle around in.

"If I meet the right woman, I'll get married," Heath said. "But I'm not forcing the issue. I'd rather be alone than make do."

Andie considered him for a beat. "Is this about your mom?"

The look he shot her was very dry. "You been watching Dr. Phil again?"

"Just because your mom didn't stick around doesn't mean that all women leave," she persisted.

"Thank you, Andie, I am aware of that." His tone was mildly sarcastic.

"Just thought it was worth saying, in case you were all bunged up about it."

He fixed his gaze on her, eyes slightly narrowed. "So what's your excuse?"

"I beg your pardon?"

"Why haven't *you* settled down and tied the knot?"

She shifted her weight, thrown by his question. "I've been concentrating on my career," she said, because it was the first thing that popped into her mind.

"You finished your apprenticeship five years ago."

"And you've dated more than enough women to find one who fits," she countered. "What's your point?"

He held up a conciliatory hand. "Okay, point taken. We're as bad as each other."

She couldn't stifle a laugh at how completely wrong he was.

"What's so funny?" he wanted to know.

"One day, when we're both really old, I'll tell you," she said.

She'd be over him by then, she figured, and her long-standing love for him would be funny.

"You keep that up, I won't tell you you've got Danish on your chin," he said.

"Where?" She wiped her chin with her sleeve. "Did I get it?"

How typical was that? He was standing there oozing sex appeal and testosterone, making her heart beat out of control, and she had food on her face. Life was not fair.

"Not even close. Here, hold still."

Heath reached out and caught her chin, his thumb brushing in a warm arc across her skin. Heat radiated out from his touch, into her breasts, down to her thighs. Flustered, she mumbled a thanks and turned away, ferrying her mug to the sink, using the small reprieve to regain her equilibrium.

She needed to get a grip. If she kept reacting like this, Heath was going to pick up on it. He might be oblivious to the fact that she was a woman, but he wasn't stupid.

"So, what are we painting?" she asked as she turned to face him again.

"Bedroom," he said.

She resisted the urge to throw her hands in the air. Now she got to help him paint his bedroom? The universe was clearly set on punishing her for her foolishness at the Valentine's Day ball.

"Let's get to it, then," she said brightly.

Chapter Six

THE FOLLOWING MONDAY, Heath pressed the end call button on his phone and glanced out the window of the job trailer. Having seen the way Andie handled the rest of the crew's ribbing this morning, he was pretty sure she would not be thrilled by what he was about to tell her. The guys had given them both a hard time when Heath had made a short announcement first thing, confirming that he and Andie were engaged, and explaining that they'd been keeping it quiet so as not to upset the status quo on-site. He'd put his arm around Andie's waist and done his best to look as though he was a happily engaged guy, but it was hard to fake it when Andie held herself so stiffly and looked so uncomfortable. Being pretend engaged was clearly not something that came naturally to her, but if they were going to get away with this, she needed to loosen up a bit.

The way she had in Grey's the other night, for example, when she'd melted against his chest and opened her mouth to him.

Not that he wanted or needed a reenactment of that profoundly disturbing moment, thank you very much. He'd had enough trouble pushing the memory away while he and Andie painted his bedroom on Saturday. As it was, he was going to feel more than a little uncomfortable next time he saw Beau, given the thoughts that had been traipsing their way through his head regarding his friend's little sister.

He exited the trailer and made his way across the cul-de-sac to the house where Andie was working. He found her in the kitchen, on her knees as she fixed the faceplate on a power switch.

"Hey. What's up?" she said, glancing up at him.

Her face was flushed, a couple of strands of hair stuck to her forehead, and it suddenly hit him that she was a very pretty woman.

Not knock-out gorgeous like a movie star, but quietly, enduringly pretty. Her nose was small and straight, her chin neat. And she had that full, rosy lower lip, the one he'd tasted so briefly on Friday night…

Andie frowned, and he realized she was waiting for him to say something. It took him another second to remember why he'd come looking for her, he was so thrown by his own thoughts.

"I just got off the phone with the *Copper Mount Courier*. Apparently when we entered the wedding giveaway we automatically agreed to a profile piece in the paper. It's in the terms and conditions."

"Are you saying we can't get out of it?"

"That's exactly what I'm saying. The woman wants us to do it tonight, if you're available. I figured we might as well get it out of the way."

Andie sat back on her heels. "Tonight?"

She looked worried.

"We'll be fine. We'll just stick to what we discussed on Saturday, take our cues from each other. Twenty minutes, it'll be over."

They'd fleshed out the details of their backstory together while they painted, and he was confident they could handle a puff-piece profile from the local newspaper without too many hiccups.

"Okay. I guess it's not like we have a choice. Did I agree to anything else when I filled out that stupid form?"

"Not that I'm aware of." He hesitated, not sure if he should say what was on his mind. "Listen. About before, with the guys. You need to relax a little if people are going to believe we're a couple."

"What do you mean? I was relaxed."

"You were stiff as a plank when I put my arm around you."

"That was because I wasn't expecting it."

"If you were really my fiancée, it wouldn't matter if you were expecting it or not. You'd want me to touch you," he pointed out.

Andie took a moment to answer, and he couldn't help noting the warm color flooding her cheeks.

"Okay. I'll work on it."

There was something in her tone that got his back up. Not that he thought he was God's gift to women or anything, but it wasn't exactly flattering to realize that a woman had to work herself up to being touched by him.

"Pretend I'm one of your boyfriends, if that helps," he said.

"Is that what you do? Pretend I'm one of your girlfriends?" Her gaze was steady on his face as she waited for his answer.

"No."

"What do you think about, then?" she asked.

He stared at her, not sure what to say, because the truth was that he thought about her. He didn't need to pretend she was someone else to feel comfortable or affectionate toward her. He liked her. He liked her a lot. He always had.

"Nothing."

She frowned, but he was saved from further interrogation when his phone rang.

"Gotta take this," he said, even though he didn't know who it was yet. "I said we'd be at the paper by five-thirty. Cool?"

He waited for her to nod before taking the call and heading for the door.

The rest of the day was busy enough that he didn't have time to dwell on the situation with Andie, and before he knew it the guys were calling out their goodbyes for the night and heading off home. He was talking through a problem with Angelo when Andie exited one of the houses. He nodded as Angelo described an issue with the drywall in one of the upstairs bedrooms, his gaze tracking Andie as she carried her tools across to her pickup. He knew for a fact that her tool chest was heavy, but she lifted it easily into the rear of the pickup before tossing in a few extra tools from her pockets. She put her hands on her hips, tilting her head back and arching her back, and he caught himself admiring the long, clean lines of her body.

She wasn't curvy, but she was elegant and strong. Willowy.

"So, what do you think?" Angelo asked.

Heath blinked, dragging his gaze from Andie and back to his employee. "Yep, absolutely," he said, nodding stupidly.

"You want me to rip it out and do it again?" Angelo confirmed.

Heath nodded. "Tidy it up, make sure the finish is right. Every house on this street will win us more contracts via word of mouth," he said. "We've got to make sure the word is good."

Angelo's gaze shifted to where Andie was securing the lock-box built into the tray of her pickup.

"You know, I thought you and Andie were trying to pull a fast one on us this morning. But I can see it now. You're a dirty dog, boss," Angelo said with a grin, punching him on the arm. "Andie's a sweetheart. You're a lucky guy."

"Yeah, I know."

Heath frowned as Angelo headed off. Andie *was* a sweetheart. Every guy on the site loved her. She could take a joke, she laughed easily, she was always ready to lend a hand. They respected her work, too. In fact, even though he had three other electricians working for him, Andie was always the one the guys wanted to work with, because she was so good at what she did.

She was also, as he'd belatedly noticed, pretty and willowy and quietly sexy.

He realized he was staring, and he turned away to lock up the trailer, deeply uncomfortable with the tenor of his own thoughts.

Beau would kill me if he knew what I was thinking.

Not to mention that Andie would probably run a mile. She nearly jumped out of her skin every time he put his arm around her. He could only imagine what she'd do or think if she knew he'd been looking at her with carnal intent.

He made a noise in the back of his throat. Even if this situation had given him a new awareness of Andie as a woman, she was not an option. End of story.

"I'm heading off now. I'll meet you in town, okay?" Andie said from behind him.

He swung around, feeling ridiculously guilty. "I'll be right behind you."

She offered him a tentative smile before walking back to her truck. He crossed to his SUV and waited until she'd completed a U-turn before following her pickup into town. They found two empty parking spots side-by-side outside the *Courier's* offices, and he waited until she joined him on the sidewalk.

"Good to go?" he asked.

"Good to go."

He offered her his hand, and Andie hesitated a moment before slipping hers into it. Together they approached the newspaper's storefront. He let her enter ahead of him, taking her hand again when they found themselves facing a tall reception counter in what was essentially an open-plan space filled with a handful of desks.

A woman was sitting at a computer workstation in the rear corner of the room, and she came to her feet and started toward them.

"Hi. I'm Marly Akers. You must be Heath and Andie. Congratulations again on being semi-finalists," she said, her smile bright as she shook hands with them both.

"It was a bit out of the blue, to be honest," Andie said, and Heath had to press his lips together to stop himself from smiling.

"I bet. I don't think the Committee considered that people's plans might change before the competition ended. Life waits for no man. Or woman," Marly said. She gestured with her head toward the rear of the office. "Come sit with me and we'll have a chat so I can work up this profile."

He squeezed Andie's hand as they followed Marly back

to her desk, and Andie shot him a swift, questioning look. He smiled to reassure her, and her face softened. Better. She'd been starting to get the deer-in-car-headlights look again.

They sat in the two guest chairs opposite Marly's desk and he settled their joined hands on his thigh. He felt Andie glance at him again, but kept his gaze on Marly, who struck him as being just as switched-on and observant as you'd expect a journalist to be.

"So, tell me how you two got together," Marly asked, her expression open and interested, her fingers poised over the keyboard of her laptop.

Andie cleared her throat. "Well, um, we've pretty much known each other since we were kids. Heath's good friends with my older brother, Beau…"

"Huh. I bet that was pretty interesting when you two started going out?" Marly asked.

Andie's head bobbed in a nod. "Yes. Beau was a little freaked out at first, but he got used to it. Didn't he?" She looked across at Heath, and he could see the uncertainty in her eyes.

She hated all the lying, he could tell. He wasn't exactly a fan, either, but they were knee-deep in this now, so the only way out was forward.

"We went out for a beer," Heath said. "I told him I was serious about Andie, and he backed off."

Marly continued to pepper them with questions, but between the two of them, he and Andie managed to field them. Andie slowly relaxed, and the three of them were laughing and getting on like old friends when Marly reached for a drawer in her desk and pulled out a small camera.

"Okay. We should probably go outside for the picture. The light's not great in here."

Andie lifted a hand to her hair. "Picture?"

"For the profile." Marly's gaze moved from Andie to Heath and back again. "I mentioned it when I spoke to Heath this morning."

Andie turned toward him, one eyebrow raised expectantly.

"Sorry. It slipped my mind," he said. "But it's no big deal. Right?"

Andie and Marly exchanged a look that Heath could only describe as 'and to think, he manages to dress himself in the morning.'

"I've got some make-up in my purse," Marly offered. "And we could take your hair down…"

Marly disappeared with Andie into the nether regions of the building, leaving Heath to entertain himself. Apparently he didn't need to worry about his hair or make-up.

He amused himself by checking email on his phone, only glancing up again when he heard the women returning.

"We can go across to the little square near the corner," Marly said as she bustled back into the room. "There's that nice old fountain there."

Heath was too busy staring at Andie to pay much attention. Her eyes seemed bluer, somehow, and her lips were shiny. Her hair was down, too, framing her face in golden waves, and instead of her McGregor Construction polo shirt, she was wearing a tight-fitting red tank top that left precious little to his or anyone else's imagination.

"I'll shoot from the waist up, so your work pants won't show," Marly said as she shooed them toward the front door.

Heath frowned as he followed the two of them out into the street, suddenly feeling as out of his depth as Andie had looked when they first came in. He'd seen Andie in her swimsuit at the lake just last year, but for some reason he felt as though he was only really seeing her for the first time. Because surely he would have noticed that she had small, plump little breasts that looked exactly the right size to fill a man's palm if he'd been paying any attention at all? And surely he would have had trouble forgetting the fine lines of her collarbone, and the way she held herself?

Then he remembered that this was Beau's little sister, and that Beau had been with them at the lake. Heath had trained himself from a young age not to let his eyes linger on Andie.

It seemed he'd been missing quite a lot.

Marly led them across the street to a small pocket park, complete with a fountain and a display of flowering annuals.

"How do you want us?" Andie asked.

"Why don't we do a simple arms-around-each-other pose

to start with?" Marly suggested.

Andie turned toward him, and he took a step closer and slipped his arm around her. Her body felt incredibly warm through the thin fabric of her tank-top, and he could feel her abdominal muscles shift beneath his hand as she adjusted her posture.

"Lovely. Now smile for me." Marly took a shot. "Why don't you look at each other this time."

Andie smiled uncomfortably as she lifted her gaze to his. He wondered if he looked half as awkward. Nothing like knowing someone was going to record your fraud for all eternity to make a guy feel self-conscious.

"You two had better get used to all the photos. If you win the big prize, there's a full photography package included," Marly said.

"Sorry. I hate photos," Andie said.

"How about this – tell me the one thing you find most annoying about Heath," Marly said.

Andie gave an uncertain laugh.

"Trust me," Marly said.

"Um, okay. Let me think…"

"This might take a while," Heath couldn't resist saying. "Andie always tells me I'm the perfect man."

"He has terrible taste in women," Andie said almost instantly.

He frowned. She shrugged a shoulder.

"Sorry, it's true."

"Until recently," Marly said.

"Right. Until recently," Andie said.

"What about you, Heath? What does Andie do that gets on your nerves?"

"Isn't this supposed to be a romantic thing?" Heath asked.

"'Humor me," Marly said.

"Right." He studied Andie's face. He honestly couldn't think of a single thing she did that annoyed him.

"There must be something," Andie said.

"She doesn't rate herself highly enough," Heath said.

"Sorry?" Andie said, blinking at him.

"It's true, Andie. You're too modest."

She scoffed. "Big Mack and I had a half-hour debate today over who was worth more to the business."

"I don't mean professionally." Heath glanced at Marly. "See what I mean? She has no idea how gorgeous she is."

Andie's mouth shut with an audible click as she stared at him, clearly thrown by what he'd said. Which just proved his point.

"That's perfect. These are going to be great," Marly said.

Heath realized she'd been snapping away the whole time he and Andie sparred with each other.

"Now, one last shot – the obligatory kiss," Marly said.

Andie gave the other woman a nervous look before reaching up and flicking her hair over her shoulder. "Okay. Sure."

She looked at Heath, then licked her lower lip. "How do you want to do this?"

"I'm thinking we'll go with the tried and true," he said.

"Wha—"

She swallowed the rest of what she'd been about to say as he lowered his head toward her, reaching out to pull her close. Despite her surprise, she slipped into his arms as though they were made for her, her face angling up to meet his. His mouth found hers, and again he tasted strawberries and something else. Something that was pure Andie, hot and female and needy.

Her breasts settled against his chest, her knees bumping his, and he was taken by surprise by the fierce surge of *want* that tightened his groin.

More than a little rattled, he broke the kiss, pulling back far enough to look into Andie's face. She stared back him, and for a second he saw the same need and heat and desire in her, and the primitive part of his brain kicked in as he calculated how long it would take him to drive to her place and get her naked.

Then she blinked and sanity returned and he took a jerky, urgent step away from her.

He was not taking Andie home to get her naked. He shouldn't even be *thinking* about it.

"Wonderful. I think that one's going to be the winner," Marly said. "Although I must say, those men you work with must be the most unobservant bunch in the history of the world not to have realized what was going on with you two."

He pulled his gaze from Andie's face. "Generally speaking, they're more interested in football."

Marly laughed, and he somehow managed to keep up a stream of small-talk as they walked back to the newspaper's storefront.

"The profile will be in next week's paper, since I've just put this week's issue to bed," Marly said. "I appreciate you both accommodating me so quickly. And good luck with the giveaway."

They shook hands, and by unspoken agreement he and Andie waited until Marly had disappeared through the door to the newspaper before speaking.

"Well, I guess we survived," Andie said, heaving a big sigh.

Speak for yourself.

"Yeah."

She dug her car keys from her pants pocket. "I'll see you tomorrow. Did you check on that conduit order?"

"It's coming first thing."

"Good. I want to do the garden lighting in number fourteen tomorrow." She gave him a distracted smile. "See you."

He walked to his own car and got in, more to stop himself from staring after her than anything else. He felt...blindsided. And it wasn't a welcome feeling. Not five minutes ago, every instinct he'd had had been telling him to get Andie into his bed, a concept that was wrong on so many different levels that he couldn't even begin to get his head around it.

And yet the need their kiss had ignited – the curiosity – still burned in his gut. And elsewhere.

Get your head out of the gutter, McGregor. This is Andie.

It was. Problem was, it was getting harder and harder to remember that.

Chapter Seven

"WEAR THE BLUE one," Lily ordered, her tone uncompromising. "It brings out your eyes."

Andie glanced across to where her friend was reclining on Andie's bed, slowly eating her way through a family-sized slab of chocolate. Lily was celebrating good news – she'd landed a new job today, which meant she could officially relax about being able to make rent.

Andie considered the t-shirt in question. "It's too low-cut."

She'd only worn the t-shirt Lily was advocating once and the whole time she'd felt as though the world was staring at her cleavage. What there was of it.

"So? You're going to a bar."

"With the guys from work. For Big Mack's birthday." Andie pulled the t-shirt off and tossed it onto the bed.

"And Heath will be there." Lily threw the t-shirt back at Andie. "Wear the blue one, Andie."

"It's too…show-offy."

"What was it Heath said again? You have no idea how

gorgeous you are. Remember that, Andie?"

Andie still felt a thrill at hearing the words, even though it had been four days since their interview with the *Courier*.

"He was putting on a show for the reporter."

"He could have said anything. He could have said that you snore or that you leave the lid off the toothpaste. But he didn't, so show off a bit, Andie."

"It's not going to make any difference."

"You don't know that. You've never tried before."

Andie widened her eyes, stung. "I have too! I've tried plenty over the years. I spent an absolute fortune on that dress for the ball."

"You should have worn red. Men are like toddlers – they're attracted to primary colors. And skin."

Andie spluttered out a laugh. Lily's views on men were half-appalling, half-hilarious.

"Heath is not a pre-schooler."

"Wear the blue top and get back to me," Lily insisted.

Sighing in resignation, Andie pulled the t-shirt back on.

"Perfect. Now, perfume. And make-up. And we have to decide what to do with your hair."

"I'm wearing it up."

"No, you're not. You're wearing it down. I just have to decide whether we should curl it or not."

Lily narrowed her eyes, clearly considering the matter.

"Don't I get any say?"

"Nope. You've had your chance. Let Aunty Lily pimp

your ride now."

Andie pretended to protest, but it was so nice to be able to talk about her feelings for Heath – finally – with someone else that she let Lily turn her hair into a tumble of loose, lazy curls. The hair help inevitably turned into make-up help, and before she knew it she was standing in front of her bathroom mirror staring at a sultry stranger.

"I can't go to the Den like this. Not with the guys from work. It looks as though I'm trying too hard."

"So?"

"No." Andie was already reaching for the box of tissues. "You don't understand, Lily. I'm not a woman at work. I'm a person. The t-shirt and hair are more than enough."

Lily must have picked up on the steel in Andie's tone because she went back to her slab of chocolate. "Okay. You're the boss."

"Now she tells me."

She did concede to one final blast of perfume before she left, taking the stairs down to the basement garage in a cloud of warm vanilla and musk. So much for ducking home briefly after work to shower before she joined the rest of the guys at the bar. Lily had turned her quick shower into a full hour of primping. The party would well and truly be started by the time she got there.

Wound up about being late, she darted through the early evening traffic as she made her way over the train tracks to the less residential part of town. Personally, she preferred

Grey's Saloon, but Big Mack chose the Wolf's Den for his party, so the Wolf's Den it was.

She found a parking spot in the Den's gravel lot, then headed up the stairs into the single-level building. The smell of beer and lots of male bodies hit her as she entered, and she quickly spotted Heath's dark head in the crowd.

Not because he was the tallest or the broadest man present, but because her internal compass had been tuned to him for too many years now. She shouldered her way to the bar before joining them, buying two pitchers of Big Sky IPA before making her way over to the table.

"Hey, Andie's here. And she brought beer," Angelo cheered as she slid the pitchers onto their table.

"Marry me, Andie," Pete said.

"Someone already beat you to it, dickhead," Angelo quipped.

Out of the corner of her eye, Andie could feel Heath staring at her. She accepted the full glass of beer Pete offered her before looking at him. He was frowning.

"What's wrong?" Then she remembered they were supposed to be engaged. "Sweetheart."

The word felt strange in her mouth and sounded even stranger, but no one seemed to notice.

"You're late," Heath said.

"We on the clock or something tonight?" She took a mouthful of lovely, crisp ale.

"I just wondered where you were, that's all." His gaze

dropped to the shadowy valley between her breasts, a geographic feature that was only possible thanks to the engineering geniuses at Victoria's Secret.

Andie went very still. She was pretty sure Heath had never looked at her breasts before. Ever. Maybe Lily had been right about the blue t-shirt.

"Stop it, man, you're freaking me out," Rory said, pretending to cover his eyes.

"He's having trouble adjusting to the new state of play," Mathew said.

Andie frowned until she realized he was referring to her and Heath's engagement.

"Well, you'd better get used to it," Heath said.

She started as his arm slid around her, pulling her close to his side. Her breast pressed against hard, masculine chest, and she hoped like hell that he couldn't feel the shiver of desire that raced through her.

"So, when is the big day? I need to mark it in my social calendar," Big Mack said.

"We're waiting to hear about the giveaway before we set a date," Heath said.

Andie smiled and nodded, hoping she didn't look as flushed as she felt. She could smell Heath's aftershave, and feel every breath he took. If he took it upon himself to kiss her right now – for appearances sake – she wasn't sure she would be answerable for her own actions.

She ducked her head, taking another mouthful of beer.

Which was when she realized her nipples were hard, two demanding peaks calling for attention in the front of her t-shirt.

Thank you, body. Way to hang me out to dry.

She angled her body slightly more toward Heath, trying to make it look as though she was simply snuggling closer when she was really trying to conceal her breasts until they got with the program and behaved themselves. Heath shifted his weight minutely.

"You okay?" he asked quietly.

"Yep. All good," she said, praying like hell that he didn't do the eye-drop thing again.

"All right. Bull's free. Who's up first?" Big Mack said, already shouldering his way through the crowd to the corner where the mechanical bull had just wound to a halt.

"I'll go," Andie said, quickly slipping out from under Heath's arm.

She wasn't a huge fan of being thrown around like a rag doll, but anything was better than a slow death from unrequited lust while pressed against Heath's side. Without looking back, she followed Big Mack into the crowd.

She could almost hear Lily's voice in her head, abjuring her to turn around and go back and make the most of this situation. She couldn't, though. She wanted Heath too much. It was as simple and as sad as that. She couldn't spend all night pretending he was hers without it doing something to her – something she probably should have thought about before she agreed to come tonight. Before she agreed to embark on this crazy fake engagement in the first place, too.

Clear thinking hadn't exactly been her strong suit lately, though. Thank God she still had an ounce of self-preservation left, because she was going to need it to get through the next few hours.

HEATH LOST TRACK of how many beers he downed as he tried not to watch Andie. Given that he couldn't take his eyes off her as she rode the mechanical bull, her long, strong thighs pressed tight to its sides, her breasts bouncing with every jerk and turn, that particular strategy hadn't exactly been a rip-roaring success.

He'd kept stealing glances at her as she played a game of darts with some of the boys, too. Hadn't been able to stop himself eyeing off her sweet little butt and the honed, lean muscles in her arms and the way she tilted her head back ever so slightly when she laughed.

If she were any other woman, he would be by her side right now, doing everything in his power to charm her. Trotting out his best lines, his best jokes. Letting her know what he wanted. What he intended.

Instead, he stood rooted by their table, an empty glass of beer in his hand and guilty thoughts circling his head.

What are you doing, man?

He had no idea. He felt as though the whole world had

been tilted, as though all the things he counted on were sliding out of his reach. The way he was feeling about Andie was insane, out of control. Wrong.

Really, really wrong. Beau trusted him. Hell, Andie trusted him. And yet he kept thinking about that moment after their kiss in the park when he'd looked into her eyes and seen lust and heat and desire.

She'd wanted him, if only for a few seconds, and that thought had been slowly but surely driving him crazy for the past few days. The way she looked tonight, with her hair flowing loose over her shoulders and her face a little flushed from beer was simply the cherry on top of his very own temptation sundae.

Go home, asshole. Take a cold shower and get some perspective.

He set the empty glass down. The voice in his head was right. He needed some fresh air and some space. He'd had enough drink to make driving unwise, and he formulated a plan as he made his way to where Andie was laughing with Mathew and Rory. He'd walk into Main Street, grab coffee and some pie from the diner and sober up some. Then he'd come back and grab his truck and drive home.

It felt like a plan. A sensible, Andie-respecting, Beau-fearing plan.

Not that he was afraid of Beau, as such. He could totally take him in a cage match. He'd just prefer not to have to.

"Andie."

She swung to face him, her face bright with laughter. "Hey."

Jesus, she was gorgeous.

"I'm heading home," he said, his tone a little more terse than he'd intended.

"Oh. Okay. Sure." She turned to the guys. "See you Monday, losers."

He frowned, then his slow brain caught up. Right. They were a couple. Of course they'd leave together. That was what couples did.

He told himself it didn't change his plan one iota as they said their goodbyes and made their way through the beer-scented dimness of the bar to the entrance. The cool night air was a welcome wake-up slap, and they paused at the top of the steps by silent mutual accord.

"That didn't go too badly," Andie said.

"Yeah." He glanced toward the parking lot. "Listen, I've got to go."

"You're not driving, though, right?" She looked concerned.

"Not yet. I'm walking into town for some pie, then I'll come get my car." He started down the steps, needing to get away from her.

She glanced at the sky. "Looks like it's going to rain to me. I can drop you home if you like."

He did not like. He didn't want to be alone in a small enclosed space with Andie right now. He didn't trust himself. Which was a pretty damn hard thing to admit, even in the privacy of his own mind. How on earth had they gotten here after only two chaste kisses and a few minutes of hand holding?

"I'll be fine," he said, just as a huge roll of thunder rumbled overhead.

Andie flashed him a grin. "Thor has spoken. Come on, grumpy bear."

She walked past him, leading the way to her pickup. More thunder sounded as he slid into the passenger seat. It would take five minutes for Andie to drive him to the two-bedroom cabin he was renting until his place was habitable. He could handle five minutes.

"Mack had a good night, don't you think?" Andie asked as she reversed out of the parking spot.

"He seemed to."

"You, on the other hand…"

"I had a good night."

"Right. That's why you had a permanent frown on your face. Is there something wrong on-site?"

"No."

She was silent for a beat as she pulled onto the road. Then she flashed him a quick glance before returning her gaze to the road.

"Are you angry with me, then?"

"No."

"You feel angry."

"What's that supposed to mean?"

"I mean you feel tense. There's a vibe."

"There isn't a vibe." If there was a vibe, it was a let's-get-naked vibe. Not an angry one.

"Okay. If you say so."

"I do."

They drove in silence for a few minutes.

"I meant to ask, do you still have my Scott rod?" Andie said. "I was thinking of doing some fishing this Sunday and I've only got my old rod at my place."

"Sure. It's in the spare room. Where were you thinking of going?"

"Not sure yet. Maybe Emigrant Bridge."

They talked fishing for the remainder of the drive, and Heath had never been so grateful for a neutral topic in his life. By the time Andie was pulling into the driveway of his rental, he was feeling back in control of himself and the situation.

He got out of the truck and climbed the two steps to the porch. He heard the thunk of the car door closing as Andie joined him and the cool night breeze sent a wash of strawberry-scented air his way as she stopped behind him.

Instantly he was thrown back to the feel of Andie's mouth hot and wet beneath his, strawberry sweet and so willing the memory alone made him hard.

So much for being back in control.

"I'll grab the rod," he said gruffly, shoving the front door open more firmly than absolutely necessary.

His gut tensed as he waited for her to follow him inside, but she remained on the porch. A small mercy. He located the rod amongst his own in the second bedroom and returned to the front porch. She was standing with her back to the door, her hair swept forward over one shoulder as she looked out into the night. The urge to simply toss the rod to one side and slide his arms around her was so strong he had to grit his teeth.

He had no right to feel this way about her.

"Here."

She turned to face him, and for a moment the curve of her cheek was limned by moonlight, pale and beautiful.

"Thanks."

She took the rod from him, then offered him a small smile.

"Hope you don't have too much of a headache in the morning. Call me if you need a lift to go pick up your car. But not too early, okay? I need my beauty sleep."

The breeze lifted a strand of her hair, and again he was breathing in the sweet smell of berries.

"What is that, anyway?" he asked, unable to stop himself. "The strawberry thing."

"My lip gloss. Why? Don't you like it?"

Her gaze held his, deep blue and mysterious in the moonlight.

"No."

"Oh. Sorry."

"I can't stop thinking about it. It's addictive."

"Oh." She lifted a hand to her lips, then thought better of it and let it fall to her side. Even though the voice in his head was telling him to back the hell up, he took a step forward.

"I'm giving you fair warning, Andie. If you don't leave this porch in the next three seconds, I'm going to break every rule I have a hundred different ways."

Her gaze widened. Then her gaze dropped to his mouth. The fishing rod clattered to the porch as she dropped it. Andie took a step forward, closing the final distance between them.

"Thank God," she said.

Chapter Eight

HEATH'S MOUTH CAME down on hers hard and hot, pushing her head back on her neck. His arms were as strong as steel as they wrapped around her, dragging her body against his. His tongue stroked hers, a demanding, urgent invasion, and she gripped first his shoulders, then his back and finally his hips as she tried to get as close to him as she could. Her whole body felt as though it was on fire, every stroke of his hands on her throat and back stoking the flames. Then his hand slid around her ribcage and onto her breast, his thumb finding her nipple with unerring accuracy, and it was all she could do not to sob out loud.

Had she always known it would be like this with him? Was that why she'd stayed fixated on him for so many years?

The thought barely had time to form in her mind before he slipped his hand beneath her t-shirt and pushed her bra out of the way, cupping her breast in his warm palm and blowing her mind utterly.

"God, Heath, yes," she panted, unable to contain herself. "*Please.*"

He pressed his hips more firmly against hers, kissing his way to her ear.

"Tell me what you want, Andie. Tell me what you need."

"You. I need you, inside me. I want your mouth on my breasts. I want everything."

Heath swore, and the next thing she knew he was kissing her again, his free hand on her ass urging her hips tightly against his. They ground together desperately, his hand doing indescribable things to her breast and nipple, his tongue claiming her mouth. He walked her backward, into his house, and together they bumped into the hall wall. He pulled at her t-shirt, not breaking their kiss until the last possible moment as he whipped it over her head, and then his gaze was raking her breasts, his eyes glittering with desire.

"*Andie*," he groaned, reaching for her with his big hands.

She arched her back, pushing herself into his palms, swallowing a sob as he pinched her nipples and then soothed them with his thumbs. Her sex felt swollen and achy with desire, and all she could think about was having him inside her, stretching her.

She reached for his belt buckle, yanking it free with shaking hands. His stud followed, then his fly, and then she was sliding her hand down his smooth, flat belly and wrapping it around the velvet steel of his erection. She stroked her hand up and down his length, her inner muscles clenching as she imagined how it was going to feel when all this leashed power was inside her.

"Andie," he said, and there was a warning beneath his words.

She stroked him again, and the next thing she knew she was on her back in the hallway, Heath looming over her, his face taut with need. He lowered his head to her breasts, pulling first one and then the other nipple into his mouth and sucking until she cried out from the pleasure-pain of it. His hands worked at the stud on her jeans, and she lifted her hips frantically as he pushed them as well as her underwear down her body. She heard the dull clink of her jeans landing on the floor as his mouth tugged at her breasts and he slid a hand over the silk of her pubic hair and between her thighs.

The first touch of his fingers on her swollen center nearly made her levitate. When he stroked her and plunged a single finger inside her she dropped her head back and started to pant.

How could anything feel this good? How could this be legal? How could she have lived twenty-six years and not experienced so much need and want and desperation?

"Andie, Andie." Heath's voice was ragged and broken, unrecognizable. "How did you get so fucking sweet?"

Something exploded inside her. She needed him right now. She'd waited thirteen years. It was enough. Too much.

She pushed him away, taking advantage of his surprise to shove him onto his back. Then she threw her leg over him and slid on top. Absolutely intent on her mission, she pulled him free from his underwear, her whole body shaking with anticipation. He was so hard yet so delicately silky in her hand as she lifted her hips and notched him into place. Her hair fell forward as she bore down on him, biting down on her lip to stop herself from screaming.

He felt so good. Amazing. So big and thick…

His hands found her hips, his eyes never leaving her face as she took him to the hilt.

"Oh, yes," she moaned, utterly overwhelmed.

The urge to move was too powerful for her to remain still for long, and she rose again, feeling the delicious slide of him inside her.

More. She needed more of this beautiful madness. His hands found her breasts, massaging, teasing, as she found a fast, urgent rhythm, riding him toward the climax that was even now bearing down on her.

It hit her like a blow, tightening every muscle, throwing her head back, loosing a keen from her throat.

"Heath. Heath," she sobbed, totally lost.

He pulled her down onto his chest, holding her close before rolling so that she was once again beneath him. Then he started to pump into her, and even though she'd thought she was done, that it was over, that there couldn't possibly be more, she felt herself tighten again.

"Please," she begged. "Yes, please."

"Stay with me, baby," Heath whispered against her mouth. "Stay with me."

His tongue stroked hers, echoing what their bodies were

doing, and she wrapped her legs around his hips and met him thrust for thrust. And then she was coming again, and he was shuddering, his face pressed into her neck, his fingers clenched into her hips as he lost himself to his own climax.

Her head hit the hall floor with a thunk as she let it drop backward, suddenly too exhausted to keep it up. She was utterly spent, breathless, her body limp and damp with sweat, the last ripples of her climax still washing through her.

Well. She'd always wondered what it would be like with Heath.

And now she knew.

God, how she knew.

HEATH WOKE TO the sound of running water. He cracked an eye, frowning. Stretched out a hand. Sure enough, the sheets were still warm beside him.

It hit him then, all of it. Andie driving him home. His warning for her to leave. Her pushing him onto his back and taking them on the wildest ride of his life.

He stared at the ceiling, waiting for regret to hit him. He'd let them both down last night, not to mention Beau. Try as he might, though, he couldn't drum up even a scrap of guilt or regret. It had been that good, that hot. That amazing.

For the rest of his life, his personal definition of sexy would be the sight of Andie riding him, her face flushed, her hair tangled around her shoulders as she gave herself over to desire. Her small, firm breasts. The lean planes of her belly. The slenderness of hefr arms and shoulders…

The water shut off abruptly in the next room. He ran a hand over his face, trying to work out how to play this. Because this was *Andie*, and what they'd done last night had the potential to cause a lot of problems, for both of them. They hadn't used a condom, for starters, that first time in the hallway. He'd managed to get it together enough the second time, when they'd made it onto his bed, but that didn't negate the first time, or the fact that she worked for him, or who Beau was in his life, or –

Andie appeared in the bathroom doorway, a towel wrapped around her torso and cinched beneath her arm. Her slender legs seemed to go on forever, and her hair hung dark blonde and wet around her face. She paused when she saw he was awake, and something flickered and then was gone in her blue eyes.

"Hi," she said.

He pushed his hair off his forehead. "Andie…I owe you an apology for last night."

She tucked the corner of the towel more firmly under her arm. "No, you don't. I had a good time. There's nothing for you to apologize for. Unless you didn't. And then I guess I should be the one apologizing to you."

The uncertainty in her tone was the only thing that stopped him from smiling. "Andie. We didn't even make it to the bedroom."

"And… that's a good thing…?"

"Trust me."

"It's just I'm not that experienced with all of this." Her gesture took in the bedroom and the two of them.

He *was* experienced, however, and there was no excuse for forgetting to use a condom last night. Something they really needed to address.

"Listen." He cleared his throat. "We need to talk about consequences."

"Consequences?" She looked alarmed for a moment, then her expression cleared. "Oh, you mean pregnancy."

"We didn't use anything that first time in the hallway."

"Right."

He watched, fascinated, as color moved up her chest and into her cheeks.

"Are you on the pill?" he asked.

"No. I'm pretty sure I'm safe, since I just finished my period a couple of days ago. But I'll go to the doctor and get some emergency contraception."

"Okay. Good." He forced himself to say the rest of what needed to be said. "I'm, um, good to go otherwise. Medically speaking. I had my annual physical a month ago."

"Oh. You mean…"

"Yeah."

"Me, too. I mean, not that it's that big an issue, since I'm not exactly, you know, *active* as such. Recently, anyway." She tucked her hair behind her ears, her cheeks very pink now. Her gaze darted to where her clothes were abandoned in the corner, and he knew she was wondering how she was going to get dressed without him seeing everything. Even though they'd practically devoured each other last night.

She was adorable. And sexy as hell. And he couldn't help thinking that even though there were a million things that could go wrong as a result of what happened last night, it would be a crying shame to ignore the fact that she was fresh from the shower and naked as a jaybird under that towel.

"You have anywhere you need to be in a hurry?" he asked.

"Did you want to go pick up your car?"

This time he didn't bother hiding his smile. "I don't give a flying fig about my car, Andie. Come over here."

Her eyes went round, then her gaze dropped to the sheet where it was pooled around his waist.

"Um. Okay."

She walked to the bed, and he crooked his finger, encouraging her closer still. She stopped when she was standing in front of the bedside table, a smile tugging at the corners of her mouth.

"Is this close enough?" she asked.

"Not by a long shot."

He reached out and fisted his hand in the fabric of her towel. Andie swallowed. He tugged gently, and she lifted her arms, loosening her grip on the towel. It came away in his hand, and he let it fall to the floor.

She was beautiful, from the delicate framework of her clavicle to the plump rosiness of her breasts to the subtle sweep of her hip and the silken hair at the juncture of her thighs. And those legs… He could still feel them wrapped around his waist as he hammered into her.

She shifted her weight minutely, enough to let him know she was uncomfortable with his scrutiny. Which was crazy, because she was utterly delicious. He came onto his knees and reached for her. She stepped into his arms, and he buried his face in the fragrant skin between her breasts.

"You have no idea what you do to me, do you?" he said. Then he turned his head and licked the side of her breast.

Her body trembled in his arms and her hands slid from his shoulders to his head, her fingers threading through his hair.

"Tell me," she said, her voice a low husk.

"You make me hard. You make me want things I shouldn't want. You make me want to lock the door and keep you all to myself." He punctuated each sentence with a lick, moving closer and closer to her nipple. It pebbled beneath his gaze, and her hips swayed subtly toward him.

"What's stopping you?" she asked.

He glanced up at her. She was watching him through heavy-lidded eyes, her mouth slightly open.

"Absolutely nothing."

Sliding his hands onto her backside, he urged her closer,

opening his mouth over her breast. She made a small, inarticulate sound as he teased the taut bud with his tongue. He slid one hand over the curve of her butt, down between her thighs, and she widened her stance as he delved between them.

She was ready for him, swollen with need. Just as it had last night, something tripped in his brain, some primitive instinct, and it was all he could do not to drag her down onto the bed and plunge inside her. He settled for kissing his way down her belly and using his hands to tilt her hips forward as he pressed a kiss to her mound. Her hands clenched in his hair, and he sensed that she was holding her breath, every muscle taut.

A wild thought occurred: she'd said she wasn't very experienced, but surely this wasn't a first for her...?

He was caveman enough that the thought turned him on. The idea that he would be the one who initiated her into this particular, very intimate pleasure was hugely gratifying, and he put his own desire and needs to one side as he pressed another kiss to the silk of her pubic hair. He delved deeper, tracing the seam of her sex with his tongue, and she trembled in his arms.

Inch by inch, moment by moment, he loved her with his mouth and tongue, pleasuring her until she was panting, her legs shaking. Then and only then did he draw her down onto the bed, sliding one hand beneath her ass as he spread her thighs wide.

She gripped his shoulder with one hand, the back of his head with the other as he feasted on her in earnest, discovering all her secrets, reveling in every moan, every twitch of her hips, every clench of her hand. She came with a low gasp, her back arching off the bed, her breathing tortured, and he kissed her thighs and belly and hips in the aftermath, savoring her satisfaction.

Her eyes were closed when he made his way back up to her breasts but they opened again when he spoke.

"Would you—"

"Yes. Please."

Her blue gaze was frankly, unrepentantly hungry, and he leaned across to find a condom in the bedside unit. Thirty seconds later, he was inside her and every thought blanked from his mind.

There was only the sound of her breathing, the warmth of her body, the taste of her skin, the sweet, crazy-making clench of her around him. He took it slow, savoring each second, waiting for her desire to build again. When she started to pant, he reached between their bodies and found her with his thumb. She came apart with a cry, her head dropping back, and he followed her, thrusting himself deep one last time.

They were both damp with sweat, their breathing ragged as they came back down to earth. He pressed a kissed to her lips, then the corner of her jaw, and finally against the soft skin beneath her ear. Even though his body felt heavier than lead, he forced himself to roll to the edge of the bed and stand. Four steps took him to the bathroom, where he disposed of the condom. Andie lay sprawled across his bed when he returned, a study in decadence and abandon. He climbed back in beside her, pulling up the sheet and duvet, and Andie shifted to the other side of the mattress.

He reached for her without thinking, drawing her back, wrapping his arms around her. She was tense for half a heartbeat, then she relaxed into his embrace, resting her head on his shoulder.

"Can I make you breakfast?" he asked after a while.

"Are we talking cereal or toast?"

"How does bacon and eggs sound?"

"Essential."

He laughed, and even though he couldn't see her face he knew she was smiling, too. The smile faded from his mouth as he registered how good she felt against him, how well their bodies fit together. He knew they should probably talk about all the complications this created in their lives, but for the life of him he couldn't bring himself to go there. This moment, right now, felt pretty freaking perfect, and he was damned if he was going to ruin it just yet.

There would be plenty of time for reality to crash around them. For now, he had Andie in his arms, in his bed, and it felt like more than enough to be going on with.

Chapter Nine

ANDIE HAD INVESTED a lot of woman-hours in dreaming about Heath McGregor over the years, but none of her fantasies had ever included leaving Heath McGregor's house in last night's clothes, her face pink from beard rash, her body tender and sore and wonderfully sated. She simply hadn't had the imagination – the experience – to go there. Consequently, it was hard to keep the smile from her lips as she slid behind the wheel of her pickup. Heath was standing on the front porch, his half-buttoned jeans hanging low on his hips, his chest and feet bare.

He looked good enough to eat, and a part of her still couldn't quite believe that she'd just burned up the sheets with him. She felt a little giddy, in fact. Almost euphoric.

She started her car and raised her hand. Heath waved back at her, then shoved his hands into the front pockets of his jeans. Even though a part of her was afraid of what was going to happen when she drove down the street and broke the bubble they'd created between them last night, she knew she needed to do it, so she reversed out of Heath's driveway and into the street, straightened up, and drove away from him.

Her brain was teeming with a million different thoughts as she drove into town, but she did her best to keep a lid on it. She stopped by the pharmacy on the way home, quickly purchasing what was required. She'd never had to use emergency contraception before, but Lily had talked about it once and she was glad she had the option. The last thing she wanted was for this situation to become even more complicated than it already was.

The giddy feeling was starting to wear off by the time she was in the elevator, heading toward her apartment. She needed another shower. And she needed to think. Get her head together. She was twisting her key in the door when Lily's door opened and her friend leapt out into the hall, a lunatic grin on her face.

"Andie Bennett, you dirty birdie. You didn't come home last night."

Andie stared at her friend, and suddenly it was all too much – the pleasure, the uncertainty, the confusion. She burst into tears, her shoulders shaking with the force of her emotion, the world becoming a blurry, inchoate mess.

"*Hey*. Andie, I was only joking. You know that," Lily said, rushing forward to put her arms around Andie.

Andie tried to speak, but couldn't get words past the lump in her throat.

"Please tell me it wasn't a huge disappointment after all

these years. Or that you spent the night in a police cell or the hospital instead of where I thought you were," Lily said, one hand smoothing calming circles on Andie's back.

"N-no. Was with H-Heath. So wonderful," Andie hiccupped.

"Ah."

Lily patted her back a few more times before easing back so she could see Andie's face. "Okay. Tissues are required, I think. And hot tea."

She hustled Andie into her apartment and put the kettle on before disappearing into Andie's bathroom and returning with a box of Kleenex. Andie blew her nose and blotted her face as her friend sat beside her on the couch.

"I would hate to be one of those smug people who says 'I told you so' at the least provocation, but I told you that blue t-shirt was rockin', didn't I?" Lily said.

Andie couldn't help but smile, even though she was feeling a little foolish now. She wasn't sure why she'd just turned into the human water sprinkler. She was over the moon about spending the night with Heath. She should be popping champagne corks and punching the sky, not bursting into tears.

"If only I'd known, I'd have worn it every day for the past who-knows-how-many years," Andie said.

"Hold that thought," Lily said, shooting to her feet and heading into Andie's small kitchen.

Andie heard the clink of mugs and the sound of the

fridge opening and closing, then Lily was back with two mugs and a packet of chocolate chip cookies.

"So," Lily said once she was seated again. "Spill."

"There's not much to tell. We went to the Den. Heath was in a really bad mood, scowling at everyone all night. Drinking more than usual. He was going to walk it off afterward, but I offered him a lift home. When we got there, he asked me about my strawberry lipgloss and warned me that I should go home because he was about to break his own rules."

Lily fanned herself. "He warned you? As in, run for your life, little girl, or I'm going to eat you alive?"

Andie could feel the heat climbing into her face. She wasn't used to talking about her sex life. Probably because it had been non-existent since Jacob. "Yes."

"Wow. That's pretty hot." Lily grabbed a cookie and bit into it, talking around the food. "You don't have to tell me any more of the gory details, it's okay. I get that this is a big deal for you. But you do have to tell me how you're feeling and what he said this morning. Please tell me he didn't do the morning-after distance thing."

"Do men do that?"

"Oh yes."

"Heath didn't. He made me breakfast."

"Breakfast is good."

Andie folded an unused tissue into a small, neat square. "We talked a little, but neither of us said anything about the future. Or if this changed anything. Or if it was more than just one night." She glanced anxiously at her friend, hoping Lily would have a brilliant insight to offer.

"Maybe he doesn't know yet. This is all new for him, remember, while you've been thinking about it for years."

"I know." She smoothed her thumb over the tissue square. "I just really want this to be the beginning of something and not the end. That's all."

Her eyes burned with a fresh rush of tears and she swallowed a few times, willing them away. Sitting on her couch crying about how much last night had meant to her was not going to change a single thing. It certainly wasn't going to miraculously change Heath's feelings. Whatever they might be.

Lily's shoulder bumped hers gently. "Go ahead and have a good cry. I won't tell anyone."

"I don't want to be sad or scared. I want to be happy. I never thought this would happen, and it did."

"But you also want more."

"I do. Does that make me greedy?" Andie asked.

"God, no. It makes you human. Heath is a great guy, and I take it from the glint in your eye he's got things covered in the bedroom department. Who wouldn't want more of that?"

Andie slowly shredded the folded tissue into strips, thinking about all the things that could go wrong, all the ways that she could wind up hurt. And yet she wouldn't change last night for anything.

"No matter what happens, I won't be sorry," she said.

"I really hope that's true, sweetie. I really do," Lily said, and Andie saw the wariness and weariness of a much more experienced woman in her friend's eyes.

The carpet in front of her was speckled with white tissue, and she leaned forward and scooped it up. Standing, she took it to the kitchen and dumped it in the trash. Then she ran the tap and wet her hands, using them wipe her face. Washing away the traces of her tears.

She'd meant what she'd said: no regrets. Last night had been wonderful. If it was a one-off…well, she would find a way to live with that. And if it wasn't…

She took a slow, deep breath. If it wasn't just a one night stand, then it would be a matter of waiting to see what it might be.

All on its own, a tremulous smile curved her lips.

She'd never realized what a scary, exciting word 'if' was before, but apparently it was going to rule her life for the next little while.

HEATH SPENT THE afternoon at the house, finishing up a handful of odd jobs and unsuccessfully trying to distract himself from thinking about Andie.

About what had happened, and how good it had been, and how complicated he'd just made his life. Three times he set his phone down, Andie's number on the screen, telling himself that he wasn't allowed to contact her again until he had a better grip on his own thoughts and feelings.

If only he could work out what they were.

If Andie were any other woman that he'd taken home from a bar and had earth-moving, awesome sex with, there wasn't a doubt in his mind that he would want to see her again. It was a no-brainer. But this was Andie. Beau's little sister. His employee. If he started something with her, it would come with a ton of strings and pitfalls attached. For starters, there was good potential for work to become weird, if not downright bad if things soured between him and Andie. Hell, that could still happen after last night. As for Beau…He simply did not want to have that conversation with his oldest friend.

The smartest, safest, most level-headed decision would be to somehow square things away with Andie regarding last night, then walk away from it without looking back.

Even though it was going to be damned hard working alongside Andie and not thinking about the warm silk of her skin, or the length of her legs around his hips, or her breathless demands for more.

Should have kept your hands to yourself in the first place, moron.

And yet he had been powerless to resist the mysterious glint in her eyes and the sweet, tangy scent of strawberries last night. Utterly powerless. In all his thirty years, he'd never felt so drawn, been so compelled by a woman.

Which was a pretty scary acknowledgement in and of itself.

He almost drew himself nuts going back and forth between his two options as the afternoon turned into night. He spent a sleepless night in sheets that smelled of Andie, only to wake in the small hours with the realization that not once in all of his brooding and pondering had he paused to wonder what Andie's expectations might be.

She had been a little on the shy side the morning-after, but hardly reluctant when they'd embarked on round three. She'd talked about Beau's business and asked questions about his plans for the house while they ate breakfast. Then she'd collected her fishing rod from the porch and gone on her way without saying a single word about what she might want or expect from him. She hadn't hinted at seeing him again. She hadn't fished for his feelings. She'd kept things light and easy and breezy.

For all he knew, she might view their night together as a fun aberration, a one-off that was never to be repeated. Or she might see it as something serious. A statement of his intentions. A game-changer for both of them.

He waited for the familiar get-out-of-Dodge feeling to kick in, the one he always got when he suspected a woman had plans for his future that went beyond next week.

And waited. And waited.

He frowned up at the ceiling. He'd told Andie only last

weekend that the only way he'd ever consider getting married was if he found the right woman. So far, Ms. Right had been playing damned hard to get, and a part of him had already been reconciled to living out his life as a bachelor. There were worse things than being alone, as his parents' messy, ugly, mean-spirited marriage and divorce had more than shown him.

But if the alternative was waking up with Andie in his bed every day…

He shook his head, genuinely astounded by his own thoughts. He and Andie had spent one night together. He had no business lying here imagining a possible future with her. No business at all. He had no idea what she wanted, and his own feelings were complex, to say the least. They might be good friends, but that didn't mean that they'd be good lovers or viable partners for each other. It was crazy to even contemplate it.

He rolled onto his belly and pushed the pillow into a more pleasing shape. The faintest hint of strawberry came to him. She'd slept on this pillow last night. She'd lain beside him, naked and gorgeous, her limbs tangled with his. The sheets had still been warm when he woke.

Then and there, he made a decision. He would talk to her tomorrow. Find out what her expectations were. What she wanted from him. If it were nothing, then he'd deal with it. If, on the other hand, she wanted more…

~

THE NEXT MORNING, Andie dragged open the door to her apartment, backpack dangling from her shoulder by a strap, cooler in hand, and stopped in her tracks. Heath stood there, hand raised as if to knock.

It took her a full second to pull herself together enough to speak.

"Hi."

He looked surprised, too, even though he at least had known he was about to see her. "Hey."

She allowed herself one quick glance down his body, taking in his plain white T-shirt, faded jeans and scuffed boots. When her gaze returned to his face, she caught him checking out her breasts, and a strange, fierce surge of heat shot through her.

Was he here for more sex? Because if he were, she would give serious thought to abandoning her fishing trip in exchange for more naked time with him. Serious, serious thought.

"I was about to head off fishing," she said, more than a little amazed by how calm her voice sounded. But maybe she shouldn't be – she'd held a candle for this man for years. She'd racked up a lot of experience hiding her true feelings from him.

"Right. I'd forgotten about that." Heath rubbed a hand over his bristly chin.

She followed the movement with her eyes, fighting back the insane, unhinged urge to lean forward and *lick* his bestubbled jaw.

"Why? Did you want something?" she asked.

Please say me naked, please say me naked, please say me naked.

"No. I mean, nothing that can't wait." He glanced down the corridor toward the elevator, but he was frowning, clearly troubled.

"I don't have to leave right this minute," she said.

"I don't want to railroad your day. I just thought maybe we should talk before tomorrow."

Right, when they'd once again be boss and employee and fake-engaged-to-be-married.

"Well…You could always come fishing with me." She hoped like hell that the invitation sounded casual and light and not desperate and needy.

His frown deepened. "I don't want to cramp your style."

"I don't have any style, in case you hadn't noticed." She waved a hand at her faded navy fishing shorts topped off by her oldest, softest flannel shirt hanging open over a black tank top. "And I've got a spare rod. If you're interested."

"Okay. As long as I'm not stepping on your toes."

"I wouldn't ask if you were," she said simply.

He seemed to relax then, his shoulders visibly dropping as he held out a hand. It took her a moment to realize he was offering to carry the cooler.

As if she suddenly wasn't up to carrying it herself.

"I've got it," she said, shooting him a look as she slipped

past him into the hallway.

They might have had sex, but that didn't mean she was incapable of looking after herself.

"Just pull the door shut behind you," she said, heading for the elevator.

He caught up with her before she got there, reaching out to hit the call button. They stood side by side in silence waiting for the car to come. Neither of them said anything on the way down, either, and it occurred to her for the first time that this was what it was probably going to be like between them for a while. Until the awkwardness of having been naked with each other had faded.

She bit her lip, then reminded herself of her no regrets rule. Friday night had been worth it, even if being uncomfortable around Heath sucked.

Heath insisted on being the one to dig the old rod out of her storage cage in the parking garage, and she waited in the driver's seat while he stowed it in the back of her pickup along with the other gear.

"I was going to grab something from the diner for lunch," she said as she pulled out of the darkness and into the bright sunshine of a late May morning.

"Sounds good."

One argument over who was paying for lunch later, she pointed the car north. The fishing spot she was aiming for was a local secret, not marked on any of the tourist maps, and after twenty minutes she turned off the highway and the car started to buck beneath them as she traversed a deeply rutted gravel track. After a few minutes she pulled into a small clearing and they both got out.

"Haven't been here for years," Heath said, looking around.

The undergrowth was thick, the taller trees casting them in deep shade, but she could hear the rushing sound of the river close by.

"I like it because I don't have to fight for fish with anyone," she said.

"Except me."

"You don't count."

He cocked an eyebrow. "What's that supposed to mean?"

"You know."

"No, I don't."

"Okay. I'll say it if you really want to hear it – I'm better at fishing than you."

Heath's head rocked back on his neck as though she'd landed a physical blow, but she knew better than to believe he was genuinely offended. He was totally playing her, and she refused to be played.

"Don't pretend you don't know it, too," she said, aiming a finger at him.

"Maybe we should have a little wager, since you're so confident," Heath said, grabbing the rods and tackle box from the tray.

"Loser cleans the fish," she suggested.

"Done."

He tucked a rod under his arm and offered her his hand. She slid hers into it and they shook, but when she tried to slip free from his grasp he tightened his grip.

"You didn't say what the winner gets," he said.

There was unmistakable heat in his dark eyes and she felt another fierce, undeniable jolt of need as she read the intent there. She swallowed, the sound audible in the quiet of the clearing. "Maybe we should leave it up to the winner to choose."

His smile was slow and loaded with dirty meaning. "I like the way you think, Bennett."

Flustered, she turned away from him. Months ago, she'd watched drunkenly from the sidelines as he smiled at his date like that at the Valentine's Day ball. At the time, she'd wondered what it must feel like to be the object of his attention and desire.

She was beginning to get an inkling of the answer: pretty damn fine.

Chapter Ten

ANDIE LED THE way along a barely discernible track through the wood, anticipation buzzing through her veins, her breathing shallow and fast. That was what Heath did to her, it seemed. Stirred her up and stole her sanity.

Soon they left the woods and walked down a gentle slope covered with long, spindly grass and dotted with the occasional shrub. A sandy bank stretched out into the water at this particular bend in the river, making it a good place to spin fish from. She glanced around briefly before settling on a spot shaded by a couple of shrubs to dump their gear. Heath squatted beside the tackle box and started searching through her lures as she pulled out an over-sized beach towel and spread it on the grass. They'd have to sit side-by-side to eat lunch, but that was just fine with her.

"Mind if I use this one?" Heath asked, showing her a lure she'd made herself a few seasons ago.

"Sure." She'd never had a lot of success with it herself, but that didn't mean he was doomed to failure.

Much.

She hid her smile, choosing her own favorite lure. They were both silent as they tied their lures to their lines. Andie opted for a Rapala knot, but she noted that Heath went with a Palomar.

Rolling up the cuffs on her shorts, she kicked off her shoes. "Your jeans are going to get pretty wet but – Oh."

Heath offered her a lazy smile as he finished unbuckling his belt. "You don't mind, do you?"

"No. Of course not."

This part of the river was hardly a high traffic area, and it wasn't as though she hadn't seen a lot more than his bare legs the other night. Still, she found herself looking anywhere but at him as he shed his jeans and boots, leaving him standing in nothing but his t-shirt and a pair of black boxer-briefs.

"All right. Let the games begin," he said, heading down to the river.

Only then did she allow herself to look at his butt, show-cased to perfection by tight stretch cotton.

Dear God. He'd better be planning to jump her again because if he was just teasing or flirting with her this was going to be the most torturous day ever.

Thoroughly distracted, she waded into the cold water, her shirt flapping around her torso in the light breeze. Heath was ahead of her, already making his first cast, and she watched as he skillfully sent the lure straight out over the water, landing with minimal splash. Immediately he began reeling in, moving the rod tip expertly. She could see the lure flashing through the water exactly like a small fish. She could also see that he had no takers.

She studied the river for a few minutes, looking for still water, and walked a little further along the bank, wading in up to her knees before casting side-arm parallel to the bank. Like Heath, she moved the rod tip from side to side, mimicking a small fish's natural swimming action. And like Heath, she came up empty by the time she'd reeled all her line back in.

She tried again, casting out a little deeper this time. Fishing was a patient person's sport, after all. Over the next hour she worked her way methodically along the section of river bank, becoming increasingly frustrated by her lack of success. She knew that Heath hadn't had any bites either, and was beginning to think they'd chosen a dud site when the sound of voices drew her gaze upstream.

A group of teenagers floated down the river on inner tubes, their laughter carrying across the water. It was a common enough occurrence on the Yellowstone, and at the height of the tourist season the river was dotted with people enjoying a leisurely ride down river.

Andie watched the boys through squinted eyes, listening to their laughter. Then she turned and studied the river downstream. There were no tell-tale flurries in the water to indicate submerged obstacles, but that didn't mean there weren't any. She eyed the boys in their tubes again, estimating their distance from the bank and how long it would take for someone to swim to their rescue should they strike trouble.

"Relax. They're all wearing life-jackets," Heath said, and she glanced over her shoulder to find him watching her.

"I know. Can't stop myself from doing the math, though."

There was a short pause as they both went back to watching the boys on their tubes.

"You never talk about him much," Heath said.

Andie frowned. Was that true? She certainly thought about Ben a lot. Every day, in some small way.

"I guess not many people know what happened."

"I know."

She nodded. Heath had been with her brother on the river that day. He'd tried to help as Beau dived over and over, trying to find Ben after he'd been knocked off his inner tube.

"'Do you think about it?" she asked.

It wasn't every day that a fifteen-year-old boy saw someone drown. That had to have done something to Heath. It had certainly had a profound effect on Beau.

"Yes." Heath considered the river for a moment. "Ben was a good kid."

"Yeah."

If she closed her eyes, she could still remember her brother's bright, brash smile, the cheeky glint in his eye, the boyish slenderness of his body. He'd been thirteen years old when he'd drowned. Far, far too young for anyone to die.

Andie hadn't been allowed to go with the boys to the river that day. At the time, she'd been furious and sulky at being forced to miss out. Afterward, she was profoundly grateful that she hadn't been there.

She hadn't witnessed Ben disappearing beneath the river's muddy waters. Hadn't seen Beau diving time after time, trying to find him. Hadn't seen the emergency workers pull her brother's pale, lifeless body onto the bank three hours later.

She'd imagined it all in her mind's eye, of course, too many times to count, but she would never know, and she suspected that was a good thing. Beau, however, had far too many vivid, technicolor details to keep the tragedy fresh in his mind.

"You think he'll ever get over it?" she asked.

To his credit, Heath didn't ask who she was referring to.

"Don't think anyone ever gets over something that big."

The tubes with their human cargo were dark smudges in the distance now, and finally she allowed herself to look away.

"You even had a nibble yet?" Heath asked.

She glanced across at him. He should have looked ridiculous, standing there in his underwear and t-shirt, but he didn't. He had amazing thighs, and lovely lean hips. And she loved the way he had just the right amount of hair on his legs.

"Nothing," she admitted.

"You want to take a break? Eat some of that cake you bought?"

"Sure. Why not?"

They waded back to shore, settling side by side on the towel. Andie passed him the take-out container holding the cake and he helped himself to a slice, immediately taking a huge bite.

"Any good?" she asked.

"Try some." He offered her a bite from his slice, and after a moment's hesitation, she leaned forward and bit into gooey, chocolatey goodness.

"Wow. That's amazing," she said, licking her lips to catch any last crumbs. It was only when she'd finished that she became aware that Heath was watching her with a fixed, singular intensity.

The heated look was back in his eyes, and something passed between them as they locked gazes.

Lust. Need. Want.

Whatever it was, it had them reaching for each other at the same time. The remainder of the cake fell to the grass as they came together, mouths open, tongues clashing. The feel of him, the taste of him was so good Andie couldn't help but moan.

"I know, baby, I know."

He pushed her onto her back, his big body coming on top of hers. She could feel how hard he was already, the steel of his erection pressing into her belly, and she ground herself against him.

He slid his hand onto her breast, teasing her through the fabric of her t-shirt, and she was instantly ready for more. For everything.

Focussed on one thing and one thing only, she started peeling his t-shirt over his head.

"Wait," Heath suddenly said against her mouth, the single word seemingly torn from him. She stilled as he pulled back enough to look her in the eye. "We should talk first. That's what I came over to your place to do. To talk."

She ran a hand over the hard plane of his chest. "Can't we talk later?"

His body tensed beneath her hand and he pressed his hips more firmly against hers. He closed his eyes for the briefest of moments, and his expression was pained when he opened them again.

"I can't believe I'm going to say this, but we should talk first," he said.

She could feel how much he wanted her, how close to the edge he was, and the woman in her couldn't help wondering what it would take to push him over. Lifting her head, she pressed her mouth to the part of his shoulder exposed by the neckline of his t-shirt, licking him with just the tip of her tongue.

"What do you want to talk about?" she asked as she let her head rest back down on the towel.

His gaze was very knowing as he looked down at her. "You want to play it that way, do you?"

She shrugged a shoulder, trying to match him for coolness.

"Okay. Two can play at that game." She felt the warmth of his hand on her belly, then the delicious slide as his hand crept beneath her t-shirt toward her breast. "I thought we should talk about what happened the other night."

His hand slid onto her breast, his thumb finding her nipple. She trembled as he teased her, her eyes not leaving his.

"All right. W-what did you want to know?" she asked, arching into his touch while at the same time sliding both hands beneath the waistband of his boxer-briefs.

"We have to work together. We're friends."

She felt him tense as she slid her hands onto the muscular curve of his butt. God, how she loved his ass.

"Is there a question in any of that?" she asked, pulling his hips closer.

His hand clenched around her breast as she started grinding herself against him, mimicking the act that she craved.

"Yes," he said through gritted teeth. "There is. I need to know what you want. What you're looking for."

"Isn't it obvious?" She ground her hips against his, forgetting to breathe when she found a particularly sweet spot.

"What about afterward? What about... more?" His cheekbones were flushed with desire, his whole body tense as he fought himself.

She knew she should be circumspect. That she should play the game, keep her cards close to her chest. As Lily had pointed out, this was new for him, even if it wasn't for her. She needed to give him time to catch up. To get with the program, if that was ever going to happen.

But he was hot and hard against the heart of her, separated from her by a thin layer or two of fabric, and she couldn't hold back.

"Yes. I want more. If you've got it to give. If you're interested. Definitely I'd like more."

"If I'm interested." Heath's voice was rough with incredulity. "Are you kidding me?"

He kissed her, his tongue invading her mouth, his hands fumbling with the stud on her shorts. Together they helped her wriggle out of them, then they took care of his underwear. At the last minute Heath leaned across and grabbed a small foil packet from his discarded jeans.

And then he was inside her, and all was right with the world. They rocked together, the only sound their breathing and the occasional word of encouragement they whispered to each other, and it wasn't long before Andie could feel herself climbing. Heath seemed to sense her urgency, his hips moving powerfully, and then she was gone, utterly gone, lost in a world of sensation. She felt him shudder out his own climax, felt the rush of his breath against her neck.

For a long moment they simply breathed, chests and bellies and hips pressed together, legs entwined. Her body felt warm and sated and heavy, and the weight of him bearing down on her was the sweetest thing in the world.

"So, I'm taking that as a yes, you're interested," she said when she was confident she could talk again without panting.

She felt rather than heard him laugh, his chest and belly moving against hers.

"You can."

"You don't want to think about it some more?" she asked.

He lifted his head and looked into her eyes. She'd been expecting amusement, but her own smile faded as she saw the serious, sincere warmth in his gaze.

"No, Andie, I don't need to think about it."

She blinked, blindsided by the intensity underpinning his words.

"Well…good."

"What about you? Do you need to think about it?"

She saw a flicker of something in his eyes, and it took her a moment to understand it was uncertainty. Heath McGregor, uncertain about *her?*

"No. I don't need to think about it. Not for a second."

His smile was sweet and maybe even a little shy as he reached out and brushed a strand of hair off her forehead.

"Good." He kissed her again, and she wrapped her arms around his shoulders and held him close.

This was so close to everything she'd ever dreamed of. That he could look at her like that, and touch her so gently, so tenderly…

Please let this be real. Please let it last.

"I have one final question," Heath asked.

"Yes?"

"You think people on the river can see my bare butt?"

She started laughing, and so did he, and she made a joke about his tan line, and he retaliated by rolling them over so that it was *her* butt that any passersby would see. She howled in protest, and they wrestled playfully before finally agreeing to get dressed and go find somewhere more private and comfortable to explore the "more" aspect of their discussion.

It only took them a few minutes to pack up, and then they were back on the road, Heath's hand heavy on her thigh. She kept shooting little glances at him out of the corners of her eyes, and every now and then he'd catch her at it and smile.

"My place or yours?" she said as she came to the point in their journey where she had to make a choice.

"Why don't we go to the Riverbend house?"

"Because there isn't a bed there?" she reminded him.

His smile was more than a little smug. "I moved into the main bedroom yesterday."

She signaled to turn right, heading back out of town. "Hope you've got food there, too, cowboy, because I plan on wearing you out."

Heath's low laughter filled the cab and she was glad she had her seatbelt on, because she was so happy, she felt as though she might float out of her seat without it. He still had a lot of catching up to do – more than a decade's worth – but for the first time she had the sense that having Heath in her life might not be as big a pipe dream as she'd always believed it to be.

Don't get cocky, Ms. Bennett. And don't you dare go letting your guard down and letting him know how you really feel. You're a long, long way from those kinds of declarations yet, and if Heath works out that this is about more than fun for you, this will no longer be a meeting of equals. Not by a long shot.

She batted the stern voice away, not in the mood for dire warnings and caution. She was with Heath, and soon they would be making love again. She figured life didn't get much better than that, even if there were unanswered questions and doubts lurking in the wings.

Chapter Eleven

"**B**OSS? YOU GONNA get that?"

Heath dragged his gaze away from the job trailer's window, focusing on Rory. Which was when he realized his phone was ringing.

"Right. Sorry. Give me a minute."

Just as he was about to take the call, his phone fell silent, a sign the call had been shunted through to voice mail. Heath made a big deal out of setting the phone down, aware of warmth flowing into his face and his foreman's curious gaze.

It wasn't the first time he'd been distracted this morning, either. He'd almost run out of gas driving to the site because he hadn't noticed the tank was low. And he'd locked himself out of the job trailer when he'd left half an hour ago to go talk to the tiler at one of the properties.

"You okay there, boss?" Rory asked, a smile lurking around his mouth.

"Yeah. Just got a lot on," Heath said.

Strictly speaking, it wasn't a lie – there were always multiple balls in the air on a construction site – but the truth was that his head was full of Andie. Memories from yesterday and last night, the scent of her skin, the feel of her body against his…

He felt like a horny, hormonal kid, desperate to see her again, constantly straining for a glimpse of her out of the job trailer window. And it had barely been four hours since they'd left his house this morning to head into work.

"So. Where were we again?" Heath asked.

"I was telling you about the problem with drainage at number 10, and you were checking if Andie was anywhere to be seen."

Rory laughed at his own joke and Heath smiled grudgingly. He deserved to be ragged on, the way he'd zoned out of both Rory's conversation *and* the incoming phone call.

"Yeah, all right. You're hilarious. Are we done here? Anything more I need to know about?"

"Nothing I can think of." Rory was still smirking, enjoying Heath's embarrassment.

"Then I guess you should get back to it."

Rory gave him a mock salute and headed for the door, whistling the wedding march as he went. Heath shook his head. Then – because he couldn't help himself – he checked out the window again.

This time he was rewarded with a glimpse of Andie as she strode across the road, ladder on her shoulder, tool kit in hand as she moved from one house to the next. Her hair was coiled in a bun high on the back of her head, leaving the elegant length of her neck bare. He had a sudden, vivid memory of kissing the delicate indent at the base of her skull this morning. Her hair had tickled his nose, and she'd squirmed against him, murmuring her approval as he slid his hand around her body and onto her –

The phone's shrill ring cut through his thoughts, startling him out of his reverie. At least he'd heard it this time. Rueful, he grabbed the handset and took the call.

"McGregor Construction, Heath speaking."

"Hi Heath, it's Jane Weiss, from the Chamber of Commerce."

He sat a little straighter in his chair. "Morning, Ms. Weiss. What can I do for you?"

He really hoped there wasn't more wedding giveaway rigamarole to deal with.

"Please, it's Jane, and I just wanted to check to ensure you and Andie can make the Summer Solstice picnic on June 21. We're trying to get as many of our finalist couples there as possible for the announcement of the winning couple."

"The 21st. That sounds okay," Heath said, making a note on the pad on his desk.

"There's a formal invitation coming in the mail, but I wanted to make sure you and Andie saved the date."

"Consider it saved."

"I ran into Marly the other day and she said your profile piece went well."

He could hear typing in the background and guessed that Ms. Weiss was multi-tasking.

"That'd be more down to Marly than me and Andie," he said, remembering the awkwardness of the interview and photo session.

"Oh, I don't know. Marly said she got a lot of good stuff from your entry form, too. Bit of a masterpiece you and Andie created there. Which reminds me, I keep meaning to mention to you that if you want to add a video or some other supporting material to your entry, you have up until the week before the picnic to deliver it. We decided it was only fair, since you two were encouraged to enter at the ball and didn't have a chance to get fancy."

Heath frowned. This was the third time that Andie's drunken entry had been praised to him. Andie had claimed she'd written a bunch of baloney, but obviously it was pretty convincing baloney or they wouldn't be finalists.

"I don't suppose you could send me a copy? We didn't get to keep one since we entered on the night of the ball," Heath fudged.

"Of course I can email a copy through. Just give me a chance to dig it out of my in-box."

"Great. I'd appreciate that."

"One last thing before I let you go. I'm going to be stepping back from things for the next little while, but if you have any queries, my sidekick, Charlotte, can answer them."

"Thanks, I'll make a note of that."

He wondered idly what would make a driven go-getter like Jane Weiss step back from a job she clearly loved. Being held at gun point? Then he spotted Andie heading for her pickup and shot to his feet. The metal steps trembled beneath his feet as he exited the trailer. Andie was standing in the tray of her pickup when he reached her, rummaging for something in the lock-box.

"Andie."

She glanced over her shoulder, eyebrows raised in question. When she saw it was him, she smiled.

"Hey."

"You in the middle of anything urgent?" he asked.

"Just the usual. Why?"

"I promised a shop owner over at the new strip mall that I'd give her a quote for a store fit-out. Want to come along for the ride?"

Andie checked her watch. "Sure, why not? It's almost lunch time. You can buy me a burger on the way back."

"Might even throw in a milk shake if you behave yourself."

"Behave myself. What does that entail, exactly?"

There was a cheeky spark in her eyes, and one hand was resting on her hip. Andie had never been shy with him, but he loved this sassy side of her.

"Exactly what you think it does."

She laughed and moved to the tail of the pickup, preparing to leap to the ground. He beat her to it, reaching for her hips and lifting her weight. Her hands found his shoulders, and he lowered her to the ground as slowly as he could manage, enjoying the slide of her body against his.

"You realize that all the guys can probably see us, right?" she said as her feet touched the ground.

"Yep." He lowered his face to hers, kissing her. Sure enough, she tasted like strawberries. "Man. What do they put in this stuff?" He kissed her again.

"Strawberries. And other things I don't want to think about." She glanced over his shoulder, clearly self-conscious, but she didn't try to leave the circle of his arms.

"You think they're giving us marks out of ten?" he asked.

She grinned, her whole face lighting up as she considered the idea. "Wouldn't that be special? We turn around and they're all holding up score cards."

He couldn't resist kissing her again. When she was smiling like that, she was utterly gorgeous and sexy as hell.

"Is this shop owner expecting you at any particular time?" Andie asked when he finally broke their kiss.

"Shit." He grabbed her wrist to check the time on her watch. "We need to motor."

Together they walked to his car. She was smiling as she pulled on her seatbelt and he started the engine. He reached for her hand, weaving his fingers with hers as he steered one-handed out of the cul-de-sac.

Her fingers flexed within his, and he shot her a glance. She was watching him, a wary, almost frightened look on her face.

"What's wrong?" he asked. "Worried I'm going to drive into a pole?"

She shook her head, her smile quickly returning. "No. I've seen you steer this thing with your knees. But maybe you should keep your eyes on the road, just in case."

He did as instructed, but the small moment stayed with him as he navigated his way through the pristine streets of the new subdivision. As well as he knew Andie – and he figured he knew her better than most people, excepting maybe Beau – sometimes he had no idea what was going on inside her head. When they were in bed together, she was pure instinct, never holding anything back. But there were moments like just now when he caught a look in her eyes and for the life of him couldn't read what she was thinking or feeling.

The really scary thing was that he wanted to know. With past girlfriends, there had been looks and glances and verbal hints that he'd been more than happy to have fly over his head. But he wanted to know what was on Andie's mind. If she was upset about something, or worried, he wanted to know about it so he could try to fix it. He wanted her to be happy. In fact, her happiness had become a priority for him in a very short space of time.

He tightened his grip on the steering wheel, wary of the way his feelings kept getting away from him. Not so long ago, Andie had been one of the crew, an old friend, Beau's sister. Now she was sitting beside him, her fingers entwined with his, and his head was full of ways to make her smile and keep her close.

It was a powerful, unnerving, tectonic shift, and a part of him wanted to put the brakes on, slow down and reassess. The rest of him was running downhill so fast that he knew there could only be one outcome when he reached the bottom.

And yet he wasn't about to let go of her hand, and he wasn't about to back away from any of this. For as long as she wanted to be, Andie was his. That was the one thing he was sure of.

ANDIE TURNED HER face into the sun streaming through the car window, closing her eyes. Heath's hand was warm around hers, the muscle of his thigh hard beneath her hand.

He'd asked her to ride along with him on a quote, just because. No sex, no hint of a bedroom, just the two of them holding hands, heading out for a quick business meeting and a burger. Like a couple. A real couple.

She opened her eyes, focusing on the world flying past, forcing herself to stay with the here and now. If she double-guessed everything and read meaning into every gesture, every invitation, every word, she would drive herself mad. It was enough that they were together, that they'd had an amazing weekend, more or less, together. More than enough.

"So, tell me about the quote," Andie said, determined to short-circuit her own obsessing.

"Not much to tell. She's new in town. Wants to open up a cafe. The real estate agent recommended us, apparently."

Andie nodded. The new subdivision was going to be home to hundreds of new families. A local place could do really well away from the competition closer to the heart of town.

"I can give you some pointers on the electrical," she said, tongue-in-cheek. "Save you from underquoting."

"Why else do you think I brought you along?"

They turned into the new strip mall, and Heath pulled up in front of one of the last remaining empty shop fronts. A slim, dark-haired woman was waiting out the front, a pair of large sunglasses shading her face.

"Lucy De Marco?" Heath said as he climbed out of the SUV.

"That's right. Which means you're Heath McGregor."

She pulled off her sunglasses and Andie felt a stab of something sharp in her belly as she watched the two of them shake hands. Lucy DeMarco was beautiful, not to mention pretty damned sexy, her curvy figure showcased by a pair of fitted jeans and a snug short-sleeved sweater.

Exactly the kind of overtly feminine, petite, dark-haired woman Heath had always gravitated toward.

Andie got out of the car and joined Heath on the sidewalk, somehow managing a smile when Lucy turned to her.

"This is Andie," Heath said.

"Hi Andie, great to meet you," Lucy said warmly.

The other woman's hand was small and soft, not like Andie's larger, work-toughened hands.

"So. You want to walk us through the site, tell us what you're looking for?" Heath said, turning toward the empty shop front.

"It's going to be a cafe, so breakfasts and lunches, no dinners. I want it to be homey and welcoming, a second home for people. I know that might be hard to achieve since this is such a new development." Lucy glanced around at the newly-minted concrete and spindly trees that had been planted in the parking lot.

"Sometimes that can work to your advantage," Heath said. "People walk in the door, and straight away they relax because you've got it right."

Lucy's smile was brilliant. "Just what I wanted to hear. Come on inside."

Andie lingered outside, allowing the two of them to go ahead, aware of the acid feeling gnawing at her belly. She'd never considered herself a jealous person before, but there was no other word for the very primal emotion churning in her gut right now.

Smoothing a hand over the top of her head, she reluctantly stepped inside. Lucy and Heath were talking at the other end of the rectangular space, Lucy's hands describing arcs in the air as she talked about a cafe she wanted to borrow ideas from back in San Francisco.

Andie couldn't help noticing how cute and small Lucy looked next to Heath. How feminine. She also couldn't help noticing that Lucy was packing a lot more up top than Andie.

Yep, definitely right up Heath's alley.

Bracing herself, she switched her gaze to Heath. He was making notes, his gaze on the pad in front of him, and when he returned his focus to Lucy, his expression was intelligent and focused, with no hint of masculine appreciation or awareness. Pretending to be checking out the space, she moved closer, continuing to watch him out of the corners of her eyes, hating herself for being so pathetic.

Heath's demeanor remained strictly professional, however, even when Lucy laughed up at him, her pretty face alight with amusement. Andie worried at a piece of cut off cable she'd stowed in her pocket, trying to work out if she was simply seeing what she wanted to see or if he genuinely hadn't noticed that his new client was a hot tamale.

"Andie, come look at these," Heath said, waving her closer.

"I was just showing Heath my inspiration pictures for Broken Eggs and Spilled Milk," Lucy explained as Andie joined them.

"Is that what you're calling the cafe?" Andie asked.

"That's right."

Andie watched as Lucy scrolled through a number of cafe

images on her phone, wondering if Heath had noticed how good Lucy smelled, and how shiny her dark caramel hair was.

She almost jumped out of her skin when a warm hand landed on her hip, jerking her gaze from the phone to Heath's face. He gave her an innocent, wide-eyed look before sliding his hand down onto her ass and giving it a light squeeze. Both actions were hidden from Lucy because of the way they were all standing, but Andie felt her face grow warm nonetheless.

She couldn't keep the smile from her face when she returned her attention to Lucy's phone, however, and over the next few minutes the gnawing feeling in her belly slowly dissipated as she absorbed a simple truth: Heath was with her. He was attracted to her, even though she wasn't small and dark and curvy. He wanted her body, he went out of his way to spend time with her. He wasn't faking it or making do until the next voluptuous brunette came along. Andie wasn't an accident or a convenience.

She was his choice.

"Come out the back and tell me what you think of the kitchen space," Lucy said.

Feeling a million times lighter, Andie fell into step behind the other woman. This time she didn't start when Heath's hand landed on her shoulder as he walked behind her. Instead, she turned her head and pressed a quick kiss to his knuckles. Because she could, and it felt right.

Chapter Twelve

TWO WEEKS LATER, Andie eased herself away from Heath's warm, hard body and slipped out of his bed. It was still dark outside, and her internal clock told her it was early. A blanket lay across the foot of the bed and she wrapped it around her naked body before walking quietly into the hallway.

The timber floor was cool beneath her feet as she made her way to the living room. The room was in darkness, but the floor-to-ceiling windows revealed a world on the verge of a new day, the horizon flushed pink with the approaching dawn. Andie sat on the floor, knees pulled tight to her chest, blanket wrapped snuggly around her huddled body. Slowly, surely, the sky caught fire as the sun rose and she rested her chin on her knees, her mind drifting back over the past few weeks.

Days with Heath at work, nights in his bed. Cooking meals with him, hiking with him on the weekends. Laughing with him. Arguing with him. Sharing silences with him.

The best weeks of her life, hands down. Nothing else

even came close. He made her so happy, sometimes she actually felt dizzy with it. A few times she'd started awake in the night, sure that it had all been a beautiful dream, that her real life was waiting for her to return to it. And Heath was always there, sleeping quietly beside her, ready to reach out with an instinctively comforting hand, drawing her close to the heat of his body.

He was so wonderful. A far better man than she'd ever realized. Sweet and tender, endlessly generous both in and out of the bedroom, he made her laugh hundreds of times a day and never failed to send her heart-rate rocketing when he entered a room.

She'd thought she loved him before, but the emotion she'd lived with for years on end was nothing compared to the way she felt about him now. Her heart – her chest – felt full with emotion, overflowing with all the things she wanted to say to him. Every day he'd do something that almost tipped her over and she had to bite her tongue to forcibly remind herself that it was far, far too early to be declaring herself to him.

When he held her close in the shower, gently washing her back.

When he offered her the last scoop of ice cream, or the final piece of chocolate.

When he met her eyes in a room full of people and smiled just for her.

There were so many moments, and each time she had to

hold herself in check and remind herself that it was early days yet. One day, she would allow herself to say what her heart wanted to say, but not yet.

The sound of bare feet on floorboards made her turn her head. Heath entered the darkened room wearing nothing but a pair of low-slung tracksuit pants, his hair sticking up on one side adorably.

"Hey. You okay?" he asked, his voice morning-husky. "I woke and you were gone."

"I couldn't sleep, so I figured I'd make these ridiculously expensive windows earn their keep."

She gestured to the orange and pink sky, and Heath spared it a glance before joining her on the floor. She started to offer him a share of the blanket, but he spread his legs and slid in behind her, wrapping his arms around her and resting his chin on her shoulder.

"You sure you're okay?" he asked after a moment.

Her heart swelled at the concern and affection she could hear in his voice.

"All good here. What about you?"

He pressed a kiss to her shoulder by way of answer, tightening his arms around her. She closed her eyes, fighting off yet another tell-him-how-you-feel urge, swallowing the words that her heart was begging to say.

Soon, she promised herself. *Soon.*

They were both silent for a while after that, watching the sky turn hazy blue and the sun resolve into a ball of yellow.

Andie was so lost in the sweet, simple contentment of the moment that she didn't register the car pulling up in front of the house until too late.

"Shit," Heath said quietly, and she knew who it was.

Beau.

Of course it was Beau. Only her brother would think it was perfectly acceptable to call on his oldest friend at the crack of dawn. Literally.

A knock sounded at the front door as Heath was disengaging himself from their embrace. She tucked the blanket beneath her armpits and let him pull her to her feet.

"You might want to go get dressed," he said.

Andie glanced down at herself. Beau had gotten wiggy when she said the word virgin and penis in the same conversation less than a month ago. She didn't want to imagine his reaction to finding her like this in his friend's home.

"You shouldn't have to face him on your own," she said, stubbornly holding her ground.

"Then dress quickly and come riding to my rescue," Heath said, grabbing her shoulders and steering her toward the hallway.

Feeling like a coward, Andie made her way to his bedroom. Thanks to the lack of furniture and soft furnishings, her brother's voice carried only too clearly when Heath let him in.

"What's my sister's car doing here?"

Andie winced at the angry, suspicious edge to Beau's

tone, dropping the blanket the moment she was inside Heath's bedroom and reaching for her clothes with urgent hands.

"Before you load your shotgun, let me explain," Heath said.

Andie clipped her bra on, reaching for her jeans.

"Unless her car is out of gas and there was some reason why you couldn't give her a lift home, I'm pretty sure I don't want to hear it."

"Andie and I are seeing each other."

Andie held her breath, waiting for her brother's response.

"Definitely not what I want to hear," Beau said.

"She's twenty-six years old."

"Don't tell me how old my own sister is."

"She's not a little kid. She's an adult."

"So, what? She's fair game? Easy pickings?"

"No. And thanks for the vote of confidence, buddy."

Andie finished tying her boots, then combed her fingers through her hair. Taking a deep breath, she went to face the music.

Both men turned to face her as she entered the living room, her boots having ensured they heard her coming. She saw at a glance that Beau was seriously pissed, his shoulders bunched, his expression hard. Heath stood a few feet away, his own expression and posture wary.

"Heath's right. I'm not a little kid," she said. "You don't need to get involved in my private life."

"You should have thought about that before you started up with my oldest friend," Beau said, his voice gravelly with anger.

"I don't need your permission to be with someone, Beau," she said.

"You really want to be a notch on his bedpost? Is that what you're all about these days, Andie?" Beau asked.

Heath started forward, chin tilted aggressively. "You might want to be careful, talking about something you know nothing about."

Any second now this scene was going to deteriorate. Andie stuck her fingers in her mouth and whistled. The sound echoed off all the hard surfaces, shrill and ear-piercing, drawing every eye to her. She aimed a finger at her brother.

"Outside, you and me. Now."

"Andie–" Heath said.

"He's my brother. I can handle this."

She didn't bother to check if Beau was following her, marching for the front door. She barreled out onto the graveled driveway, crossing her arms over her chest and turning to face her brother as he exited the house.

"What are you playing at, Andie?" he said, getting straight into it as he stalked toward her. "You want to end up on the scrap heap of women Heath McGregor has fucked and forgotten?"

Andie glared at him and said the only thing she could think of that might shut him up: the truth.

155

"I love him."

Stunned, Beau rocked back on his heels.

She lifted her chin. "I've loved him since I was thirteen years old, and there's an outside chance he might just love me, too, so don't you screw this up for me, Beau."

She expected Beau to fire back at her with some counter-argument or other, but instead he closed his eyes as though she'd just delivered him a fatal blow.

"Andie. God." His eyes were dark with sympathy when he opened them.

"Don't look at me like that. I'm not an object of pity. It's not pitiful to love someone."

"You've known Heath half your life. You've seen what he's like with women. How many of his girlfriends do you think have been convinced that there was an 'outside chance' Heath was going to love them back?"

"I have no idea. It doesn't matter. This is me. This is different."

"*Andie.*" He sounded pained.

"You don't know him like I do," she insisted.

"No, I know him like *I* do. I've been in bars with him. I've heard him talk about women."

"So? I bet you talked right back at him about your women. Does that make you a bad bet?"

"Hell, yeah it does. I wouldn't want my sister with someone like me, not in a million years. And that's exactly who Heath is."

"Beau, you cannot protect me from this. I love that you want to, but you can't."

"He's going to hurt you, Andie."

"Maybe, but that's my risk to take, not yours."

Beau looked down the driveway, his expression hard, the tendons in his neck tight.

"Is it so impossible to believe that he might love me?" she asked quietly.

Beau's head snapped around, his gaze narrowing. "This isn't about you, Andie, okay? You are gorgeous, you are smart. I'm so goddamned proud of you I'd shout it from the top of Copper Mountain if I thought it would make a difference to anything. One day you're going to meet a guy who sees all of that. But I don't think that man is Heath McGregor." There was a dead, flat certainty to her brother's tone that struck a chill in her heart. "I'm sorry, Panda, but it's the truth."

She turned away from him, looking out over Riverbend Park, rubbing her arms against the early morning cold. Trying to think. Trying to see clearly.

Had she been fooling herself, living in a fantasyland where she got to have the handsome prince of her dreams, when in fact she'd simply had his body on loan for a few short weeks? Had she been reading meaning into Heath's affectionate touches, freighting them with more emotion than they really held? Or was the feeling she got when she was with Heath as good and true and real as she hoped it was?

She thought back to the moment they'd just shared, the warmth of his body around hers as they watched the sun rise. That had been about more than sex. She was almost certain of it. Almost, but not quite.

Heath had always been affectionate toward her, after all. If she'd asked him before that first kiss, she was sure he'd have said that he loved her before all this started – as a friend. Maybe what she was sensing was a mixture of old affection and new lust. Maybe her brother was right, and she was just weeks away from becoming one of Heath's exes.

The thought made her chest ache and her eyes burn.

"I don't want you to get hurt, Andie," Beau said.

She smiled grimly. "Your timing is a little off on that one, I'm afraid."

She glanced toward the house. She could see Heath standing in the living room, watching them, his expression unreadable from this distance. Suddenly the thought of going back inside and talking to him with her brother's doubts ringing in her head was just too much. She needed to think. She needed some space and distance to get her head on straight.

She turned to her brother and held out a hand. "Can I have the keys to your truck?"

"I'll drive you home –"

"No. I want to be alone. My car keys are on the kitchen counter. We can swap back later."

Beau studied her a moment before pulling his keys from his pocket and dropping them into her open hand.

"Tell Heath I'll call him later, okay?"

She didn't wait for him to respond, and she didn't look toward the house as she crossed to her brother's SUV. Her stomach in knots, she started the car and threw it into gear. The tires grabbed with a spurt of gravel, and she pressed her fisted hand into her sternum, refusing to cry as she headed down the drive.

She'd told Lily and herself that even if nothing came of her one night with Heath, she would never regret it. She wasn't sure she could stand by that declaration now. If Beau was right and her heart wrong, her whole world was about to collapse in on itself. She'd have to find a new job. She'd have to boycott all of Heath's favorite places in town. She could never go fishing or camping or hunting with Beau and Heath again.

Not to mention the small fact that her heart would be smashed to smithereens, too.

She was trembling as she pulled onto the highway heading toward town. Afraid of the depth of her own feelings, terrified of the disappointment and hurt she could already feel lapping at her ankles.

He might be wrong. Heath might love you. There's no reason why you can't be The One.

She wanted to believe the voice in her head, she really did, but she'd endured so many years of standing on the sidelines, watching Heath with women who were more confident, more sexy, more alluring than her. The truth was, Heath had only noticed her when she'd practically shoved herself down his throat, and he hadn't said a single word in all their time together about his feelings or the future.

All of which made it really, really hard to hold onto the precious, fragile dream of his love.

A single tear slid down her face and Andie brushed it away with the back of her hand. Now was not the time to cry. Now was the time to be smart, to protect herself, and to think.

HEATH WAS ALREADY heading for the front door when Beau let himself in.

"What did you say to her?" Heath demanded. "What did you say to make her drive off?"

"The truth. That you aren't a person she should count on."

Heath swore, barely resisting the urge to charge at his friend.

"You really think I'd hurt Andie? You think I'd do anything to make her unhappy?"

"If you felt that way you should have kept your pants zipped."

Heath made a rude noise, disappointed and disgusted in equal measure. "You know what? I'm not explaining myself to you. Andie's the only one I owe anything to."

Beau walked past him, heading for the kitchen.

"You want to tell me where the hell you think you're going?" Heath asked. He and Beau had been through a lot over the years, but Beau was really pushing it right now.

"Andie said her keys were on the kitchen counter."

Heath arrived in the kitchen in time to see Beau scoop up the keys to Andie's pickup. Andie's wallet was there, too, and her phone. Beau went to pick them up, but Heath spoke first.

"I'll get those to Andie."

Beau ignored him, setting the phone on top of the wallet and picking both up. That was it for Heath, the one step too far that tore his restraint to shreds. Moving fast, he got in Beau's face, stopping just short of slamming into him.

"Whether you like it or not, Andie is a part of my life, and she's going to stay that way. So you'd better deal with whatever's stuck in your throat pretty damned fast because I'm not going anywhere."

Something flickered behind Beau's eyes, and for a second he hesitated. Heath took advantage of the moment, taking Andie's things back. His heart was pounding, adrenalin pumping, and he moved back a few paces.

"She's not your property, Beau."

"She's my sister."

"She's also a person."

They eyed each other for a long beat. There was more

Heath could say – like how freaking disappointing it was that his best friend thought he was such a sack of shit that he wouldn't let him date his sister – but he knew there was a lot at play here. Ever since Ben's death, Beau had made the role of older brother a sacred calling. This was about more than Heath and Andie.

"Shut the door on your way out," Heath said, turning away.

He was halfway to the bedroom when he heard the door slam shut. He tossed Andie's things onto the bed, frowning at the tangled sheets.

Why had she driven off like that? What on earth had Beau said to make her want to bail without even looking Heath in the eye?

It was tempting to think that Beau had aired some dirty laundry from Heath's past, but Andie knew him. He'd never hidden his private life from her, she knew his history, and she'd entered into a relationship with him with open eyes and arms. She'd come willingly, eagerly into his bed, in fact.

"Screw it."

He shed his tracksuit pants in one smooth move, striding to the bathroom. Five minutes later he was showered and brushing his teeth, and five minutes after that he was in the car, heading into Marietta. He wasn't going to sit around second guessing what was going on. He was going to talk to Andie, ask her outright, and they would work out whatever was wrong, remove whatever block Beau had put between them.

Because he'd meant what he said – he wasn't going any-where. Andie had slotted into his life as though she was made for it over the past weeks, filling the space by his side, occupying vacancies in his life that he hadn't even known were empty. He loved being with her. He loved the sound of her laughter. He loved the way she moaned when he slid inside her. He loved her down-to-earth practicality, and the way she never backed down from a fight.

No way was he letting her go. No way was he losing the best thing that had ever happened to him. Not when they were just at the very beginning of what might be possible between them.

He came to a stop at a traffic light, drumming his fingers on the wheel impatiently, aware of a hollow, jittery sensation in his gut.

He was nervous. The truth was, he had no idea what Andie wanted. It was all very well for him to be so gung-ho, for him to want what he wanted, but he had no idea if she'd just been in this thing for fun and it had become something else, or if it was still simply about great sex for her, or –

Someone leaned on their horn behind him and he real-ized the light was green. He raised a hand in apology, stepping on the gas. He was about to turn off Main Street when his phone started ringing. He hit the button on the steering wheel to take the call.

"McGregor Construction," he said automatically.

"Boss, it's me," Big Mack said. "We've got a problem at the site. How far away are you?"

Heath frowned. "What sort of a problem?"

"Four of the houses have been ransacked. They've smashed windows, stolen tap fittings, stripped out pipe and wiring…"

Heath swore. They were insured for this sort of thing, but it was beside the point. They'd need to reglaze windows, redo plumbing and wiring. They could be looking at a major setback, which meant they'd go over time on the builds and trigger the penalty payments built into the homeowners' contracts…

Checking the rear view mirror, he did a sweeping u-turn. "I'm five minutes away, tops. Have you called the cops?"

"They were going to be my second call."

"Get onto it, and I'll see you shortly."

Heath ended the call, swearing again and punching the steering wheel. Talk about a crappy morning. He'd have to deal with this mess before he could even contemplate sorting things out with Andie, something that simply didn't sit right with him. He hadn't been able to see her face clearly when she was talking to Beau, but there wasn't a doubt in his mind that she'd been upset when she'd left his place.

Damn Beau to hell.

Chapter Thirteen

HEATH LEFT SOME rubber on the road when he screeched to a halt in front of the job trailer. Big Mack and Angelo were waiting for him, their faces grim.

"Cops said they'd be here in half an hour," Big Mack reported.

Heath jerked his head toward the houses. "Show me the damage."

He did a quick tour of the four houses that had been targeted, noting the walls that had been punched through to access plumbing, the missing vanities and fittings in the bathrooms. Fortunately the kitchens had not yet been installed, but light fittings, switches, cabling had all been stolen. Shaking his head, Heath headed back to the trailer, Big Mack and Angelo hard on his heels.

It was obvious that the thieves had tried to smash their way into the job trailer, too, but the heavy-duty pad bolt and lock had defeated them, and the window was too elevated to offer them easy access. No doubt the houses had been easier and more lucrative targets.

"I want you guys to go through each house and make a detailed list of everything that's missing. Check inside walls, the roof spaces, the basements. Take photographs, make sure you've got it all down. The insurance company will want to do their own audit, but we need to start documenting and ordering replacement supplies."

He turned on his computer, his mind racing.

"We're going to have to split the crew in half, get some of the guys working on repairs, keep the other half moving forward on the untouched properties. I'll see if I can get a few extra guys in."

"Little Mack's in-between jobs right now, right?" Angelo asked, glancing at Big Mack for confirmation.

Big Mack's younger brother was also a builder, and he'd helped Heath out in the past on odd jobs here and there.

"Yeah, he's around," Big Mack confirmed.

"Great. Call him, ask if he can start immediately," Heath said.

His computer came to life and he clicked through to his insurance folder as the guys armed themselves with notepads and pens and turned to go.

"Work fast, guys," he called after them, and Angelo and Big Mack raised acknowledging hands before disappearing out the door.

Heath punched in the claim number for the insurance company and ground his teeth together when he got a recorded message with instructions to select options that would guide him through the insurance company's call center. Two minutes later he was on hold, waiting for "the next available customer service officer".

Frustration building, he started scanning through the emails that had come in overnight, automatically deleting the marketing spiels. He paused when he came to one from Marietta Chamber of Commerce, clicking through. It was an apology from Jane Weiss for having forgotten to send him a scanned copy of his and Andie's entry in the wedding giveaway. Curious, hold music still playing in his ear, Heath clicked on the PDF attachment.

Andie's handwriting filled the screen, small and neat, and even though he knew the police were due to arrive any minute and that he had a dozen things that needed doing *now*, he started reading.

Describe how you and your fiancé first met: Heath McGregor and I have known each other since we were kids. For a long time there he was just my oldest brother's cool friend. And then, one day, overnight it seemed, he became something more. I don't know what it was, and I never did anything about it, because he was my brother's best friend and because I didn't think he'd be interested in someone like me. That all changed last year, though, when we went camping together. My brother was supposed to go, but he pulled out at the last minute and it was just Heath and me. We found a site by the river and spent the day fishing and talking. That night, we sat around the fire and shared a bottle of wine and talked some more. It started raining sometime in the night, which was when Heath's tent started leaking. He came looking for shelter in my two-man tent, and…well, let's just say it turned out that we'd both been sitting on some strong feelings for each other…

HEATH STARED AT the screen, trying to understand what he was reading. Andie had said she'd written a bunch of baloney for her entry, but she was describing a real camping trip he'd taken with her and Beau last year. They'd set up camp by the river, as she'd written. They'd fished all day and sat around the fire talking into the night. It had rained, and his tent had leaked – but he'd sought shelter in Beau's tent, not hers.

Perplexed, he kept reading.

Tell us a bit about the groom (hint: we suggest the bride fills out this part!): Heath is one of the smartest people I know. He's worked incredibly hard to build his own business, and every day I see how good he is with people, how he makes them want to work hard for him. He's a natural leader, decisive, calm. He's also kind, and thoughtful, and he's never too busy or too stressed to notice the little things. He makes me feel important, like I count, and he listens to what I have to say. Once, for my birthday, he gave me a tiny apple pendant on a gold chain because I mentioned that I missed the apple tree in my parents' backyard. He's not perfect, don't get me wrong, but he's a good man with a big heart, and I know he's going to make a wonderful husband and father.

Heath shifted uneasily, uncomfortable with Andie's vision of who he was. She knew his failings better than anyone – how short tempered he could get sometimes when he was frustrated, his annoying perfectionist streak when it came to the small details, his stubborn refusal to admit when he was wrong sometimes. Yet Andie had painted him with a generous brush, highlighting his better characteristics, ignoring or accepting the lesser. As for the apple pendant... He'd given that to her on her eighteenth birthday. More than eight years ago.

Tell us a bit about the bride (hint:we suggest the groom fills out this part!) Andie Bennett has been part of my life for a long time, but it wasn't until we went camping together that I really saw her. She'd tell you she's not the most beautiful woman in the world, but she's beautiful to me. She's shy sometimes, but I know that's just because she doesn't want to push herself forward. She's super-smart, and any man can tell you that's a huge turn on. When I'm with her, the world feels right. As though all the pieces fit. I thank the Universe every day that Beau couldn't make that fishing trip, and maybe one day I'll tell Andie that I cut a hole in my tent that night so I'd have to share with her.

Heath sat back in his chair, momentarily blown away by what he'd just read. What he'd just realized.

Andie hadn't written a load of baloney, she'd written a wish list. She'd written the world and their relationship the way she wanted them to be. She'd offered up her vision of Heath, and described the way she wanted him to see her – as beautiful and smart and precious.

She loved him.

He shook his head as half a dozen things suddenly made

sense. Her paralyzed embarrassment when Jane had come to inform them of their semi-final status. The way she'd ripped into Sharon after his ex had belittled Andie's appeal as a woman in Grey's Saloon. Andie's discomfort with holding hands and casual touching before they became lovers. Her comment about him having bad taste in women during the interview with the local newspaper. Her never-ending generosity toward him, his business, his interests...

You idiot. You enormous, whale-sized idiot.

He bowed his head, momentarily overwhelmed by his own stupidity. How could he not have seen it? How could he have lived with her by his side, beneath his nose, for half his life, and not understood her heart?

More importantly, how could he have wasted so much time? Caused her so much pain? Over and over again...

The many, many times he'd introduced her to one of his girlfriends as "practically his little sister". The times he'd called her "kid" and refused to notice she was a woman. The times he'd accepted her company, her friendship, her generosity as everyday occurrences, commonplaces, when in fact they'd been gifts, precious gifts, from a woman who deserved so much better.

An image came to him – Andie's pale, taut face as she spoke to Beau in front of his house this morning, her arms crossed tightly over her chest. As though she was defending herself against a blow.

He shot to his feet, reaching for his keys. Three strides

took him to the door; he practically vaulted down the steps.

"Boss. Where are you going?" Big Mack called as Heath raced to his SUV.

"I need to see Andie."

"What about the cops?"

"You handle it."

Heath slammed the car door, cutting off whatever Big Mack had been about to say. He was vaguely aware of the other man stepping aside, his mouth slightly agape, as Heath hot-footed it out of there.

The mess at the site could wait. Andie couldn't. She'd been waiting years for him to wake up. He refused to make her wait another second.

The drive into the old part of town seemed to take forever, and he leaned forward over the steering wheel at every set of red lights, willing them to turn green. He threw the SUV into the first parking spot he saw, racing into Andie's building. The elevator was too slow for him; he took the stairs two at a time, barreling through the fire door on her floor. His heart pounding in his ears, he knocked on the door. When she didn't answer immediately, he knocked again. When there was still no answer, he swore and pushed his hair off his forehead. It was seven in the morning. Where in hell could she be?

Think, idiot. She was upset. Where would she go if she was upset?

Normally, he'd think of Beau, but that was obviously out

of the question today. He ran through half a dozen options before admitting he had no clue. Frustrated beyond measure, he descended to ground level and exited the building. He was heading back to his car when the security grille to the building's underground garage rose with a mechanical whine and Beau's SUV drove out. Andie sat behind the wheel, her eyes hidden behind a pair of sunglasses, a cap pulled low over her face.

"*Andie.*"

The car started forward and he ran toward it, pounding on the rear fender seconds before she accelerated into the street. The SUV lurched to a stop and he walked to the driver's window. There was the smallest of hesitations before Andie slid it down.

"What are you doing here?" she asked, clearly surprised.

She was wearing a McGregor Construction polo and her work pants, and it hit him that she was heading for the work site.

Of course she was. Andie would never let him down by bailing on work simply because she was upset.

"Can we talk?" he said.

"If this is about what happened this morning, I'm sorry. I shouldn't have taken off like that, but Beau just pissed me off so much I had to get out of there." She said it lightly, with just the right undercurrent of annoyance in her tone.

If he hadn't read the entry form, he might have bought it – she was that good at hiding her feelings from him. And why not? She'd had plenty of years to fine-tune her technique.

Without saying a word, he reached out and pulled her sunglasses from her face.

"Hey," she protested, but it was too late. Her eyes were a tell-tale red, the skin around them slightly puffy.

She'd been crying.

The realization was like a punch in the gut.

He opened the car door. "Get out of the car."

"Heath."

He reached in and unclipped her seatbelt, then physically hauled her out of the car and into his arms. Her body was tense, resisting, for the first few seconds, then she relaxed into his embrace.

"I'm fine," she said quietly. "I was just upset with Beau."

How many of these little white lies had she told over the years to shield her feelings from him? It killed him to think about her hiding herself from him like that.

He tightened his arms around her, pressing a kiss to the top of her head. She was so damned special, this woman who had quietly loved him without asking for anything for herself for far too long.

"I read your entry in the wedding giveaway, Andie" he said.

She tensed. "What?"

"I asked Jane for a copy and she emailed it to me overnight."

She pulled free from his embrace, her face creased with confusion. "Why did you do that? I told you it was a load of baloney."

He held her eye. "I wish you'd said something. I wish I'd pulled my head out of my own ass long enough to realize. I'm so sorry, Andie…"

Her eyes widened, the blood draining from her face. Then she took a step back, shaking her head.

"Don't apologize to me, Heath. And don't you dare feel sorry for me."

"I don't. Of course I don't. Andie – Jesus, I'm doing this all wrong. I should have said it last week, or the week before, but I didn't want to rush you. Which shows how dumb I am. I love you, Andie."

ANDIE STARED AT him, then she shook her head again, backing away from him this time. "No, no, no. Don't do this. Don't you even *think* about doing this, Heath."

This was her worst nightmare: Heath finding out that she loved him and being freaking *noble* about it. He was that kind of man. He paid his taxes. He honored his debts. He stood by his friends. He'd ridden to her rescue not once but twice after she'd sucked them both into the vortex of the wedding giveaway. Of course he was going to do the right thing now that he knew how she felt. Of course.

Heath caught her arms, halting her retreat. "I love you,

do you hear me? I love you."

"This is why I never said anything to you. This is exactly why. I knew you'd feel guilty, or honor bound or some dumbass thing like that. I knew you'd try to do the right thing. I knew it."

Her eyes burned with unshed tears but she was determined to hold her ground. After an hour's fierce thought in the privacy of her apartment this morning, she'd come to the conclusion that she had no choice but to continue with her relationship with Heath, even if that meant playing it out to the bitter, painful end that her brother had predicted.

She loved Heath and craved being with him too much to walk away from him.

But that didn't mean she was prepared to accept his pity or his guilt. She might have nursed her feelings for thirteen years, but she still had her pride and her dignity.

"You think I'd lie about the way I feel about you, Andie? About how important you are to me?" Heath's face was tight with the intensity of his emotions. "That night I kissed you and we never even made it to bed, I was terrified I'd messed up one of the best things in my life, but that was the smartest thing I ever did, Andie, because it was the beginning of us."

She stared at him, wanting to believe, but it was too perfect. Too convenient. Too close to her dream. The plain-Jane girl only got the guy she'd loved from afar in the movies. In real life, she missed out and made do.

Heath's grip tightened on her arms. "I might be slow,

baby. I might be the most unobservant, undeserving man on the face of the earth because I didn't work it out sooner, but once I had you in my arms I knew I didn't want to let you go. I knew that it was right, and that everything would be wrong without you from that moment on. I knew that I didn't want to imagine a future without you in it."

He cradled her jaw in his hand and looked into her eyes. "I see you, Andie. I finally see you, and I adore you. I'm nuts about you. I want you to move into the house with me and make it a home. I want us to get married. I want us to do the whole family thing. I want it all, Andie, because you're the only person it will ever make sense with."

His mouth found hers and he kissed her, cradling her face in both his hands. His kiss was both tender and demanding, and she realized that he was trembling with the force of his feelings, all six foot one of him. Something broke loose inside of her then and she opened her mouth beneath his, her hands fisting in the fabric of his t-shirt as she drew him tightly to her.

Because only a fool would make do when the man she loved was offering her the future she wanted. And Andie had never been a fool.

She kissed him as though it was the last kiss they'd ever share, as if time was about to end, as if she only had this one precious, perfect moment to share with him. And he kissed her back, his arms hard as steel around her, and it sank into her bones that this was real, that he meant what he was saying, that he wanted her.

He loved her.

He really loved her. After all these years, he was finally hers.

"Tell me you believe me," he said as he kissed his way across the slope of her cheek to her ear. "Tell me you want the same things I do."

"You know I do." Her hands were aching, she was grasping his t-shirt so fiercely.

"Then marry me, Andie. Let's turn this fake engagement into a real one, because I don't want to waste another second of my life without you."

For a moment it was all too much. His love, his proposal, the future he was offering her. She'd bounced from huge doubt to this in the space of a couple of hours. She was overwhelmed. Overloaded.

He swallowed, his Adam's apple bobbing nervously as he waited for her answer, and she saw the uncertainty in him, the hope, and it hit her that this was just as big a moment for him as it was for her. Suddenly he was simply Heath, the man she'd known almost her entire life, and the comfort and serenity and certainty she'd felt this morning as she watched the sunrise in his arms washed over her.

The doubts her brother had fanned into flames blew away like dust, along with thirteen years of never being the one. She loved this man, and he loved her. Whatever else they had to work out between them they could muddle through along the way.

Her mouth curved into a smile as she looked into his eyes. "Yes," she said. "Yes, I'll marry you, Heath McGregor."

Because what else could she possibly say?

He wrapped his arms around her, pressing his cheek to hers. "Thank God. I love you, Andie."

"I love you, too, Heath. So much."

Thirteen years she'd waited to say those words, and they flew from her lips so easily, so naturally.

His arms tightened around her. "You have no idea how good it is to hear you say that."

"You have no idea how good it is to say it."

"Say it again."

"I love you."

He pressed a kiss to the angle of her jaw. "Again."

"I love you."

He kissed her ear lobe. "More."

"I love you. I love you. I love you."

He punctuated each declaration with a fresh kiss, finding her temple, the tip of her nose, the slope of her shoulder. She laughed, tilting her head obligingly as he found new places to anoint, and the floating-away-with-happiness feeling gripped her again.

"Do you ever have the feeling that a moment is too good to be true? Like you're watching it in a movie, or maybe it's a dream?" she asked him impulsively.

He took his time answering, his gaze scanning her face

with loving intensity. "Only when I'm with you."

She closed her eyes, savoring his words, savoring the buoyant, warm expansive feeling behind her breastbone.

This is the first moment of the best of my life, she thought.

Opening her eyes, she looked at the man she was going to marry, the man she'd loved for half her life, and she kissed him.

Maybe some moments were too good to be true, but that didn't mean they weren't real.

Chapter Fourteen

ANDIE HEFTED THE picnic hamper, listing a little to one side with the weight of the thing.

"We packed way too much food," she said.

Heath reached out and pulled the hamper from her hand. "We'll see."

She grabbed the waterproof picnic blanket and her car keys. "That wasn't a challenge."

"I know, but I'm a man of big appetites." He wiggled his eyebrows.

"Now, *that* feels like a challenge."

"Feel free to take me up on it anytime."

She laughed, and he used his body to back her against the counter before lowering his head to kiss her. She let the blanket fall to the floor, reaching up to grip his big shoulders, giving herself over to the moment.

It had been twelve days since he'd declared himself on the sidewalk in front of her apartment building, and every day he showed her in new ways how much she meant to him. True to his word, he'd insisted she move into the

Riverbend house, and now her few pieces of furniture dotted the otherwise empty rooms, dwarfed by the scale of the home he'd built. As Lily had dryly pointed out, they weren't going to win any interior decorating awards, but Andie didn't give a flying fig.

She was living with the man she loved, waking up in his arms every morning. As far as she was concerned, they could be living in a shack in the middle of a swamp and she'd still be giddy with happiness.

"What time does this picnic shindig start, anyway?" Heath asked as he lifted his head, his dark eyes glinting with intent.

"Half an hour ago."

"Plenty of time."

He lowered his head again, but she laughed and held him off. "We're the guests of honor, remember?"

He sighed and rested his forehead against hers. "Okay. But only because I owe the Chamber of Commerce for coming up with the wedding giveaway scheme in the first place."

"How do you figure that?"

He dropped one last kiss onto her lips. "Because otherwise it might have taken me longer to see what was right under my nose."

"I would have gotten sick of waiting at some point and just pounced on you," she said confidently.

In truth, she owed the anonymous woman who had

handed her the entry form at the ball an enormous debt of gratitude.

"Maybe we could practice your pouncing technique when we get back from the picnic," Heath suggested.

As usual, the gravel in his tone and the heat in his eyes did crazy things to her insides and she reminded herself forcibly that it would be really, incredibly rude if they didn't turn up at the picnic.

"Stop leading me into temptation, McGregor," she warned him, scooping up the picnic blanket on her way to the door.

"Can't help it. You inspire me."

He caught up with her at the pickup, and she tossed him the keys and slid into the passenger seat. He started the truck, put it into gear, then caught her hand and brought it to rest on his thigh, his own hand settling warmly on top of it. Something he almost always did when they drove together these days. Just one of many little habits of affection that had developed between them.

Andie glanced at him, and her heart literally ached with all the love she felt for him. He had two days' worth of stubble on his jaw and his hair needed a trim, but he was easily the best-looking, sexiest man she knew, and one day soon, he would be her husband.

Her awareness of his love – her faith in it – was still new enough that the knowledge sent a thrill through her and made her feel a little teary, but she was long past the point where she doubted the sincerity of his feelings. It was impossible to hold onto her fear when he loved her so well, so fervently, so sincerely. The way he looked at her, the way he spoke to her, the way he made her happiness the burning priority of his life...

"Where are we meeting Lily?" he asked as they headed into town.

"Near the statue." She snuck a quick glance at him. "Beau's joining us, too."

Heath didn't say anything, but there was a subtle change to his posture and she knew he was mentally climbing onto his high horse. Now that they were real-engaged and not fake-engaged, he wanted Beau to eat his words along with some serious humble pie. Beau had other ideas – ever since Heath's proposal, her brother had stubbornly refused to say anything except offer her and Heath a terse congratulations.

She figured he'd come around once Heath asked him to be best man. Of course, Heath would have to realize he *wanted* Beau to be his best man first, which might take some time. It was tempting to interfere, but Andie wasn't about to meddle in a friendship that was almost as old as she was. It was up to the men to sort their issues out.

The west end of town was busy, the streets lined with cars, and Andie guessed the Summer Solstice picnic was going to be counted as a success by the powers that be. The many picnic blankets dotting Bramble Park confirmed her guess, and she and Heath waved to acquaintances as they made their way toward the statue commemorating the copper miners that had been so important in the foundation of Marietta.

Lily and Beau were waiting side by side, both looking less than pleased to be in one another's vicinity. Andie sighed inwardly. This was either going to be the kind of day that healed rifts, or the kind that became legendary for its awkwardness. At the moment, her money was on the latter, but she was holding out hope for the former.

"Hey. Sorry we're late. Heath couldn't decide what to wear," Andie said.

Heath responded to her blatant lie with a grin, well aware she was trying to goad him. "Nice try."

Andie hugged Lily, feeling a pang of guilt over the fact that they hadn't had a good girly catch-up since things had taken off with Heath. She absolutely refused to become one of those women who lost contact with her girlfriends because she'd become half of a couple, and she gave Lily an extra-firm squeeze before letting her go.

"We need to have a margarita night," she said.

"You know where to find me," Lily said. Was it Andie's imagination or was there a flicker of sadness in her friend's eyes?

"This week. You pick the night," Andie said.

"Wednesday, since it's hump day?"

"Hump day it is."

Andie turned to her brother next, noting that he and

Heath were doing the strong, silent thing instead of catching up the way they normally would.

Yep, it was going to be an awesome afternoon.

"Thanks for coming," Andie said, kissing his cheek.

"Figured I was lucky to get an invitation," Beau said.

Heath threw him a sharp look, and Andie's hopes for the day took an upturn. Maybe her brother wasn't going to be as stubborn as she'd suspected he might be.

"Where do we want to sit?" Andie asked.

"I already reserved us a spot near the bandstand," Lily said. "'Figured you'd want to be close for when the big announcement is made."

Andie rolled her eyes. "We are so not going to win."

Lily and Heath exchanged a quick glance and Andie narrowed her eyes.

"What do you two know that I don't?" she asked suspiciously.

"Nothing. You think Jane would allow anyone to steal the thunder from her big announcement?" Heath said.

Andie wasn't entirely convinced by his innocent routine but Lily was leading the way toward the blanket she'd spread out to the left of the bandstand. A jazz trio were playing – not Andie's favorite form of music, but for some reason a perennial at outdoor events – and they spread out her and Heath's blanket next to Lily's and unpacked a bottle of wine and some glasses. Her bother hovered for a couple of minutes before joining Lily on her blanket, carefully keeping well away from her.

For the first time she seriously considered Lily's contention where Beau was concerned. Did he really disapprove of her because he knew she'd once been a stripper? Her brother had never struck her as being judgmental or a prude, but there was no getting around the fact that he simply wasn't his normal, relaxed self when he was around her.

"Who wants wine?" Heath asked. Everyone did, and Andie occupied herself with handing out glasses while Hearth poured.

"To Andie and Heath," Lily said once they all had a drink. "May you always be this happy and this in love."

Andie got a little misty-eyed when her friend produced a gift from her tote bag and passed it over.

"Don't get too excited. It's not a Lear jet or your own private tropical island," Lily warned.

"You shouldn't have. We don't need gifts," Andie said. Having Heath was more than enough for her.

"It felt like something that needed to be documented," Lily said, her smile bordering on cheeky.

Andie gave her friend a bemused look before tugging at the ribbon and peeling the paper free. Inside a layer of tissue paper was a beautiful reclaimed oak frame, and inside the frame was a clipping of her and Heath's profile piece in the Copper Mountain Courier.

"Oh. I missed this," Andie said, glancing up to give Lily a grateful smile.

"I thought you might have."

A color picture accompanied the article, one of the shots Marly had taken near the fountain in the little pocket park. Marly had caught her and Heath in a moment of laughter, and Andie's chest got a little tight as she saw the expression in Heath's eyes as he looked at her. He looked charmed and amused and a little bemused, as though someone had just hit him on the back of the head with something hard and heavy and he was feeling a little dazed. She passed the frame to him and watched the slow, acknowledging smile curl his mouth as he studied the photo.

"Pole-axed," he said, glancing across at her.

She grinned. "Didn't know what hit you."

"You can say that again." He set the frame carefully to one side and looked at Lily. "Thanks for our first family heirloom."

"My pleasure."

Andie noticed that Beau kept glancing across, trying to catch a glimpse of the image, and she passed it to him wordlessly. His face was expressionless as he studied the image and read the article, but he shot Heath an assessing look when he'd finished.

"What?" Heath asked.

"You look like you've got a head injury," Beau said.

Andie almost snorted her wine out her nose. "*Beau.*"

"A head injury," Heath said thoughtfully. "I was thinking it looks more like I've just been hit by a tranquilizer dart.

The type they use at the zoo when an animal escapes."

A smile tugged at the corner of Beau's mouth. She glanced at Heath. He was doing the trying-not-to-smile thing, too.

Men.

"Why don't you two just kiss and make up? Save us having to watch you flirt with each other all afternoon?" Lily said.

"Only time I'm kissing Beau is if he needs CPR," Heath said. "And even then I'd think twice."

"I don't need to think twice," Beau fired back. "You'd be shit out of luck if the situation was reversed."

This time their smiles were more pronounced, and Andie settled back against the warmth of Heath's chest and heaved a silent sigh of relief. Apparently there was not going to be a huge family rift and endless stags-locking-horns action between her husband-to-be and her brother. Definitely a load off.

"Hello. Looks like we've got a bit of action going on up on the bandstand," Lily said.

Andie glanced across and saw that the jazz trio were setting their instruments aside to make way for Jane Weiss and the mayor, Maynard J. Gleeson.

"I see Maynard has bought himself a new waistcoat," Heath said.

Marietta's mayor was known for his colorful waistcoats. Today's was a vibrant mustard-yellow, an unfortunate choice for a man with more than a little ginger in his hair.

"Good afternoon, everyone," Jane said, her voice booming over the speakers. "It's so lovely to see so many of you enjoying the sunshine at the Summer Solstice picnic. Don't forget that we will have live music all day and into the night. The party goes on! But before we enjoy the next band, we have a rather wonderful task to perform – announcing the winners for Marietta's Great Wedding Giveaway competition. This has been such a rewarding exercise for so many of us involved in the giveaway. We had the chance to read so many stories of cute meets and perfect proposals…"

Andie caught Heath's eye, remembering how all this had begun – her foolish ramblings at the Valentine's Day ball, Sharon's feral attack in the saloon, Heath's kiss to save Andie's pride. It had been a roller-coaster ride, but it had been worth it. Heath smiled and shifted so that he could wrap his arms around her from behind. Secure in his arms, Andie refocused on what Jane was saying. As Heath had mentioned earlier, having benefited from the giveaway in the best possible way, it seemed only fair that they be here to congratulate and celebrate the winning couple.

"…I can assure you there were tough discussions within the judging panel. But there was one couple that we all felt captured the spirit of the giveaway more than any other. Maybe it was their heartfelt entry, or the video the groom provided. Or maybe it's just because they make a fabulous couple, and we can't wait for them to have their happy ever after. Everybody, please join me in congratulating the winners of Marietta's Great Wedding Giveaway....Heath McGregor and Andie Bennett!"

The crowd clapped and whistled, heads turning toward where she and Heath were sitting. Andie frowned, not quite understanding.

"Did she... Did Jane just say our names?" she said, twisting to see Heath's face.

He was grinning, and she swung back to see that Lily and Beau were grinning, too.

"She did just say our names!" Andie said. "Oh my god. Ohmygod. We won. *We won!*"

"Heath and Andie, can we get you to come up here so we can all get a good look at you love birds?" Jane called from the bandstand.

Heath stood and Andie followed suit, grinning but confused now that her brain had kicked in.

"But...we didn't have half the stuff the other entries did," she said. "No photographs or playlists or videos. I hope there hasn't been some kind of mistake."

"Well...There may have been a video." Heath winked at her.

Andie blinked. "But how did you – Why would you – I'm confused."

"I did the camera-work," Lily said, putting up her hand. "Heath was the talent and the editor."

"When did you do this?" Andie said, staring at the dark

horse she was about to marry.

"Remember that quote I was working late on last week?"

"Why did you do this?" Andie tried again, baffled. Filming a video… It was so out of character for Heath, she didn't even know where to start.

"Jane offered us the opportunity to add one to our entry, since we entered at the ball. And you know my competitive streak," Heath said.

"Better shake a tail feather. That woman from the Chamber of Commerce looks like she's about to come hunting for you," Beau warned.

Still grappling with the news that Heath had made a video, of all things, to augment their entry, Andie allowed him to lead her to the bandstand.

"Here they are, everybody. Andie and Heath," Jane said.

The Mayor stepped forward to shake their hands, and Jane kissed and hugged them both. Andie was surprised to see a sheen of tears in the other woman's eyes, and to feel the genuine warmth in her embrace.

"I'm so pleased it was you two," Jane whispered in Andie's ear.

"I'm sure we'd all like to hear from the happy couple," Mayor Gleeson said.

Heath glanced at Andie, and she shook her head adamantly. No way was she taking the mike and talking to a park full of people she barely knew. Heath accepted the microphone, drawing Andie under his arm as he faced the crowd.

"Well, I think it's pretty obvious that we're blown away. We didn't expect to win, but it's a great surprise and we want to thank the Marietta Chamber of Commerce and all the businesses and craftspeople, who have donated prizes. We'd especially like to thank Jane Weiss, who has been our go-to person through all of this. Most importantly, I want to thank Andie, who entered us in the giveaway in the first place. The best idea you ever had, sweetheart." Heath pulled her closer, and before she knew it he was kissing her, right in front of everyone.

Andie could feel herself blushing, but she kissed him right back. She figured she would always kiss this man back, as long as she drew breath.

The crowd hooted and hollered as they ended the kiss, and Heath held their joined hands in the air before handing back the microphone. The Mayor said a few words to wrap things up and introduce the next band as Andie and Heath descended the stairs to ground level. Marly was there from the *Copper Mountain Courier*, her camera in hand, and Andie's eyes widened as she registered the gentle swell curving the front of the other woman's shirt.

"Yep, that's right, I'm pregnant," Marly said with a smile.

"Congratulations," Andie said.

"Thanks. We're pretty excited." Her gaze found a tall, dark-haired man Andie recognized from around town.

"Great news. Congratulations, Drake," Heath said, stepping forward to shake the other man's hand.

They exchanged a few words, then Marly took some shots of them with Jane and the Mayor. Throughout it all, Andie kept a lid on her burning curiosity, but the moment they were on their way back to the blanket and out of earshot, she grabbed Heath's arm.

"What video?" she asked.

Heath simply smiled and slid his phone from his back pocket, calling up something on the screen before handing it over. An image of him filled the screen, with an arrow watermarked across his face, and she hit the arrow to start the video.

"My name is Heath McGregor," Heath said on the screen, his gaze admirably steady as he stared down the barrel of the camera. "And I want to talk to you today about the woman I'm going to marry, Andie Bennett."

The screen changed to a shot of an apple tree, but it wasn't until the camera pulled back that Andie realized it was the apple tree in her parents' former home on Collier Avenue. He must have asked the current owners for permission to film in their yard.

At least, she hoped he had.

"You're looking at this apple tree because this is where I first laid eyes on Andie Bennett. She was six years old, and she was way up high in the branches when her brother, Beau, brought me home from school. Even then she was one of the bravest people I know. I never told her this, but even though

Beau and I climbed all the way to the top of the tree to check out the view, I was freaking out every inch of the way. But no way was I going to let on that I was scared in front of a girl, so I sucked it up and made out as though I climbed trees like that every day."

Andie smiled, then shot a look at Heath and found he was watching her with a warm, watchful intensity. She returned her gaze to the screen, but caught his hand in hers.

The screen shifted to a shot of the Yellowstone River, the camera panning to take in a wooded hillside before finally finding the snow-capped peak of Copper Mountain.

"This is where Andie and I used to go camping together with her brother when we were teenagers. Another thing I'm never going to admit to my wife-to-be – she can out-fish me any day, in any conditions. I'd appreciate it if that could be our little secret."

"You need to look up the definition of 'secret'," she said, not taking her eyes from the screen. Heath squeezed her hand.

"For a long time there, Andie was just my best friend's little sister," Heath said on the video. "I loved her like my own sister, in fact, and it took me a while to work out that the brave kid who could out-fish and out-climb me had turned into the hottest, most beautiful woman in Marietta."

Andie shook her head.

"If Andie was standing beside me right now, she'd be shaking her head at that," on-screen Heath said. "She has no idea how fine she is. My plan is to spend the rest of our lives making sure she does know."

The camera zoomed closer to Heath's face, and she was looking straight into his dark chocolate eyes as he spoke, it seemed, directly to her.

"Andie, your faith in me, your friendship and your love are the most precious gifts I've ever received. I hope like hell that I'm worthy of them. I love you, sweetheart."

The video ended, and Andie swallowed the hot lump of emotion in her throat. A tear plopped onto the screen, and she felt Heath's hand on her chin as he tilted her face toward him.

"I wasn't exactly aiming for tears," he said.

He'd gone to so much trouble, and not because he had a competitive streak, as he'd claimed. He'd done it for her.

"I love you," she said. "I love you so much it hurts."

"I know, baby. Believe me, I know."

She turned into his embrace, burying her face in his neck, her arms tight around him, breathing in the good, strong smell of him. He held her just as tightly, hands splayed wide on her back. After a moment she was able to let him go, sniffing back the last of her tears.

Heath tucked a strand of hair behind her ear, his eyes gentle on her face.

"So, Ms. Bennett, what do you say we go plan our wedding?"

She smiled slowly. "That sounds like a mighty fine plan, Mr. McGregor. Mighty fine."

Epilogue

Barely a month later...

A NDIE SLIPPED HER arms through the spaghetti straps as the cool satin of her wedding dress slithered down her body.

"Just let me get the zip," Lily said, and Andie held her breath as her friend tugged at the back of her dress. She'd known the moment she tried it on in the pretty dressing room at Married in Marietta that it was her dress. Her chest had gotten tight, and she'd suddenly been so excited for the big day to come that she almost couldn't stand it.

Wait till Heath sees me in this, she'd thought.

And now that moment was but minutes away.

"Okay. You can look now," Lily said.

Andie turned to face the mirror. For a moment, she was so taken aback she couldn't speak. This morning, she and Lily had spent a couple of hours at Nell's Cut 'n Curl having their hair fixed by Rainey Brown, who was nothing short of a hair genius. Andie had been impressed with the way Rainey twisted her hair into a loose bun and pinned it to one side of her head, creating a charmingly asymmetrical look that made the most of her slim neck. Now that the hairdo was combined with her dress and full make-up, however, she didn't quite recognize the woman in the mirror.

Her dress was made from ivory satin with a sweetheart neckline and a gauzy, lacy over-dress embroidered with daisies and other wildflowers. A sheer lace panel rose up from the sweetheart neckline to cover her chest, supported by two slim straps, while the A-line skirt flowed from a natural waist, making the most of her willowy figure.

"You look beautiful," Lily said, awe in her voice.

Andie took a deep breath and said something she'd never said before in her life. "I do. I do look beautiful."

Lily made a triumphant sound and punched the air. "That's my girl. You own it, Andie."

Lily scooped up the pearl earrings Beau had bought Andie for the occasion, helping her fasten them. Andie watched her friend's attentive face in the mirror, well aware of how much care and time Lily had poured into her and Heath's wedding planning over the past month.

It had been a crazy, hectic time, with every single evening for the past month being dedicated to some aspect of the big day or touching base with one or other of the businesses or people who had offered prizes for the wedding giveaway. There'd been a meeting with Laurent Fletcher, who was making them a full bedroom suite from locally sourced recycled timbers, and another with Beck Hartnett, who was hosting their reception at Beck's Place, his restaurant on the outskirts of Marietta. There'd also been a meeting with The Copper Country Band to go over the music for the reception, an in-depth discussion with Risa from Sweet Pea Flowers about the bridal bouquet, fittings for her dress and Heath's suit, practice runs for her hair and make-up with Rainey…

Andie's head spun just thinking about it, and Lily had been with her every step of the way.

"Before we go, I have something for you," Andie said, reaching for her handbag. She pulled a small velvet pouch from the side pocket. "This is to say thank you for everything, especially the insanity of the past few weeks. You're my rock, Lily, and I wouldn't be standing here without you."

Lily made a dismissive gesture but she was blinking rapidly, obviously worried about ruining her make-up. Andie watched as Lily pulled the delicate gold chain and pendant Andie had chosen from the pouch. Made by local artisan, Bailey Jenkins, the pendant was a gold and sapphire rendering of a Mariposa Lily, the stone at the center a perfect match for the deep blue-purple of Lily's floor-length sheath.

"Oh, it's gorgeous," Lily said. She fanned her face and Andie laughed.

"No crying today. We made a pledge."

"As if we're going to be able to stick to it. Andie, thank you. I love it. Will you help me put it on?"

Lily turned her back and Andie slipped the chain around

her neck and fastened the catch.

"There. I think we're both done," Andie announced.

For a moment they stopped and stood side by side, studying their reflections in the mirror.

"Men are going to weep," Lily predicted. "'They're going to gnash their teeth that you are off the market, Andie Bennett, soon to be Andie McGregor. But I will be waiting to comfort their tears."

Andie grinned at her friend's bravado. She knew for a fact that Lily hadn't stepped out with a man for months, part of the "man sabbatical" she'd imposed on herself.

"We'll see," Andie said.

They spent another few minutes double-checking lipstick and spraying on perfume, then they left the bedroom and made their way to the living room where Beau was waiting to drive them to the church, Heath having been banished to Beau's place last night. Her brother looked pretty damned breath-taking in an ivory tuxedo with white shirt and black tie, a prefect match for Heath's suit.

"Wow," Andie said. "Don't you scrub up okay, if it's not creepy for a sister to say that about her brother."

"I was about to say the same," Beau said. "You look beautiful, Andie."

He wore a proud smile, and she was so thankful that he had set aside his concerns and embraced her new relationship with Heath. She had no idea if he and Heath had ever formally cleared the air – she suspected it wasn't their way to hash things out the way she and Lily might have – but they certainly seemed to be back on their former footing. If anything, they might even be closer.

Beau's gaze went to Lily. "You look lovely, too," he said politely.

Her smile was just as polite. "Thank you."

Andie frowned, but today was not the day to tackle their apparently mutual antipathy.

"Your chariot awaits, madam," Beau said, waving her toward the door.

Andie lifted her skirts and walked carefully out to his SUV, picking her way across the gravel driveway and sliding into the back. Lily got in beside her and they exchanged small, excited-but-tense smiles.

Beau fired up the engine.

"Wait. Did you put the flowers in the car?" Andie said suddenly, leaning forward to grab her brother's shoulder as he started to pull away from the house.

"They're in the back," Beau said.

"And you've got the rings?"

"You sound like Heath. Yes, I have the rings."

"Okay. Then I think we can go."

"Thank you," Beau said dryly.

Andie held Lily's hand all the way into town, her belly getting more and more tense as they approached St. James Church. Beau pulled up out the front and her father exited the huge double doors, hurrying down to open the car door.

He and her step-mother had arrived in town yesterday. His smile was wobbly as he helped Andie exit the car.

"You're stunning, sweetheart. So beautiful."

"Thanks, Dad."

"Your mother's in the vestibule. She was worried the wind would take her hat," he explained.

Andie glanced at the entrance and saw her mother waving from inside, the wisp of pale pink silk and straw on her head a match for her floral dress and matching long jacket. According to her mother, she'd scoured all of Miami before she found the perfect mother-of-the-bride ensemble. Andie waved back, then accepted her bouquet from Lily. Risa had crafted a beautiful, relaxed bouquet of peonies and pale lavender David Austin roses, all bound with a pale lavender ribbon, and Andie took a moment to close her eyes and inhale its fragrance.

So many people had told her that her wedding day would fly by in a blink, and that tomorrow she would be complaining how it was nothing but a blur, but she was going to do her best to make as many memories as she could on this special day.

Consequently, she took a moment to look at her father, taking in the pride in his eyes, as well as Lily, who was blinking like crazy now, trying to stave off tears. Beau had already slipped into the church to take his place beside Heath at the head of the aisle. She tilted her head to admire the bright blue sky and fluffy white clouds overhead, as well as the weathered stone of the church's façade.

Then she took in a deep breath, and let it out.

"Okay. I'm ready. Let's go find my husband," she said.

Her father offered her his arm, and they walked into the vestibule where her mother got emotional about how pretty Andie looked. Lily passed over some of her secret stash of tissues, and they waited until Andie's mom was calm again before throwing open the doors to the church proper. The organist took her cue, and the first strains of the wedding march filled the church. Heads turned in a rustle of clothing and hushed murmurs, but Andie's gaze was only for the man at the head of the aisle. Heath looked almost shockingly handsome in his ivory tuxedo, his hair tamed for the occasion, and his gaze was loaded with private meaning as it met hers down the long aisle.

I love you, his eyes said. *I can't wait to make you mine.*

Lily started up the aisle, each step in time to the music, and after a few beats Andie followed, a parent on either arm.

Heath watched her every step of the way, and she could tell by the way he kept swallowing that he was fighting strong emotion. She could sympathize – her chest felt three sizes too small for her heart, and she had to quell the urge to simply run into his arms.

Finally she reached the head of the aisle, and Father Kincaid began to speak.

He asked who gave Andie into marriage, and both her parents announced that they did, stepping away and allowing her to take Heath's hand. His fingers closed over hers, warm and sure and strong, and Andie looked into his eyes and saw her future and her past and her present.

This was the man she would spend the rest of her life with. The man she would make children with, God willing. The man she would grow old and mellow with. The man who would protect and support and challenge and love her every day.

The man she loved, the man she had always loved.

It was so easy to say the words when the time came. It felt as though she'd been waiting years to say them, and in many ways she had. Holding both Heath's hands in hers, looking into his eyes, she offered up her vows.

"I, Andie Eloise Bennett take you, Heath Adam McGregor, to be my lawful husband, to have and to hold, from this day forward, for better, for worse, for richer, for poorer, in sickness and in health, to love and to cherish until death do us part, according to God's holy ordinance, and therefore I pledge thee my faith."

Ten minutes later, her secret, most cherished, most private and special dream became a reality as they were announced husband and wife. Heath didn't stand on ceremony – he pulled her into his arms, kissed her with unseemly but very welcome desire, and spun her around in a dizzying circle.

They were both laughing when he set her back down on her feet, and Andie knew that there would be many more years of laughter and love ahead of them, because this man wasn't just her passionate, avid, intense lover, he was also her trusted, gentle friend.

"Ready?" he said.

"Always."

Hand in hand with her husband, she turned to greet the world.

THE END

More Books by Sarah Mayberry

Love Sarah Mayberry? Add all of her contemporary romance titles to your shelf!

Almost a Bride

Bound to the Bachelor

His Christmas Gift

Available now at your favorite online retailer!

THE GREAT WEDDING GIVEAWAY

The excitement is building in Marietta, Montana, with a series of stories centered around the 100th Anniversary of the Graff Hotel and – as part of the celebration – an incredible Wedding Giveaway…

Available now at your favorite online retailer!

ABOUT THE AUTHOR

Sarah Mayberry is the award winning, best selling author of more than 30 books. She lives by the bay in Melbourne with her husband and a small, furry Cavoodle called Max. When she isn't writing romance, Sarah writes scripts for television as well as working on other film and TV projects. She loves to cook, knows she should tend to her garden more, and considers curling up with a good book the height of luxury.

Visit her website at www.sarahmayberry.com.

Thank you for reading

MAKE-BELIEVE WEDDING

If you enjoyed this book, you can find more from all our great authors at TulePublishing.com, or from your favorite online retailer.

TULE
PUBLISHING

Made in the USA
Monee, IL
15 August 2023

41086024R00132